"Go ahead and kiss me," Holly said matter-of-factly.

Steven raised his brow. "Now?" Trusting honey eyes mesmerized him. Why hadn't he noticed them before tonight?"

"What better time?" she murmured, standing on tiptoe to put her arms around his neck. "It's so noble of you to offer to teach me to please a man . . . isn't that what you promised?"

He didn't feel noble at all. He felt hot with a sensual awareness. He wanted to rip off her pink dress, feel her soft skin come alive under his hands, hear her throaty voice moan that she wanted him. "Are you sure?"

She threaded her fingers in his hair, then kissed the side of his neck with nibbling love bites. "Yes, very," she said softly.

He stared down at her for an endless moment. Whatever game she was playing, it took two. His mouth found hers in a branding kiss. If she had started out by teasing him, she was soon caught up in her own design. Her kisses were sweet torture, sweet madness, and she could never have enough. . . .

WHAT ARE *LOVESWEPT* ROMANCES?

They are stories of true romance and touching emotion. We believe those two very important ingredients are constants in our highly sensual and very believable stories in the *LOVESWEPT* line. Our goal is to give you, the reader, stories of consistently high quality that may sometimes make you laugh, sometimes make you cry, but are always fresh and creative and contain many delightful surprises within their pages.

Most romance fans read an enormous number of books. Those they truly love, they keep. Others may be traded with friends and soon forgotten. We hope that each *LOVESWEPT* romance will be a treasure—a "keeper." We will always try to publish

LOVE STORIES YOU'LL NEVER FORGET
BY AUTHORS YOU'LL ALWAYS REMEMBER

The Editors

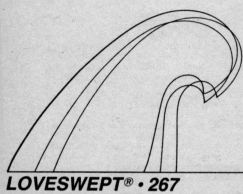

LOVESWEPT® • 267

Doris Parmett
Made for Each Other

 BANTAM BOOKS
TORONTO • NEW YORK • LONDON • SYDNEY • AUCKLAND

MADE FOR EACH OTHER

A Bantam Book / July 1988

If you would be interested in receiving protective vinyl
covers for your Loveswept books, please write to this address
for information:

Loveswept
Bantam Books
P.O. Box 985
Hicksville, NY 11802

ISBN 0-553-21910-3

Published simultaneously in the United States and Canada

Dedication

To Roberta Galli, Chris Heggan, Dot Brown, Mildred Fedorka, and Sheila Tart, for their warm support and friendship;

to Stan Helfman and Bob Heggan, for cheerfully answering technical questions on moratoriums and land use;

to my agent, Sharon Jarvis, for her faith;

and to Buzz, who knows why.

One

"Memorize his face. Dig up every bit of gossip, inside information, and dirt you can about Steven Chadwick," ordered Daniel "Digger" Danville. "Search his garbage if you have to!"

An eight-by-ten glossy sailed across the famous Hollywood gossip columnist's cluttered desk and landed on the lap of his new research assistant.

The suntanned face of the man in the picture stared up at Holly Elizabeth Anderson. It did not even remotely look like the face of a man who wanted his garbage searched. If anything, his firm-set mouth, his dark brown hair, his slightly arched dark eyebrows, his nose—which could be termed a trifle too long—and his piercing blue eyes seemed to be daring her to try searching through his belongings, even his discarded belongings.

Her sudden chill had nothing to do with the

horrible summer cold she had caught a week ago and which seemed to have taken up permanent residence in her system. Her head felt as if it were being squeezed inside a bandbox, her raspy throat was raw from coughing, her eyes smarted from the high concentration of smog polluting the Los Angeles basin, and her nose resembled Rudolph the Reindeer's. Holly dug into her skirt pocket for a tissue. She missed the clean, fresh air of Minneapolis.

Her index finger covered up one of Steven Chadwick's menacing blue eyes. "Why can't I make an appointment to interview him? Robin Leach doesn't poke in garbage pails!"

Digger affected a disdainful tone. "True." He traced a manicured fingernail along the flat top of a metal letter opener. "Robin skims the surface. He satisfies the whim for opulence. I, on the other hand, intend to delve deeper." Enthralled with himself, the wiry little man popped forward. "I'm going to give women the brass ring. Utopia! A *how-to* guide! A road map on finding and landing America's most elusive bachelors." He peaked a shrewd blond eyebrow meaningfully. "With your help, of course. That's why I hired you."

His not-too-subtle meaning drifted across the desk. Holly's sinuses might be clogged, but her brain wasn't. This was not the prudent time to remind him she had originally been hired to research a "where-are-they-now" type of book dealing with the lives of yesteryear's legendary movie stars. With no warning, he had changed her assignment. What hadn't changed was her need to pay the rent on her small but expensive North Hollywood apartment. Besides, she had to admit that the new assignment, if handled correctly, could be exciting, and that's why she'd come to the West Coast.

Digger charged off his chair, thrusting his small hands upward in a power salute. "Women, bless their spendthrift little hearts, comprise over fifty percent of the population. Sex-starved, marriage-minded women who'd kill to get their hands on a man like Steven Chadwick. Even if one percent of them buy my book, I stand to make a fortune."

Of all the chauvinistic claptrap! Digger's composite sketch of her sex took the cake. She, for one, wouldn't be caught dead purchasing a book on how to snare a rich bachelor. It smacked of the hunt, pure and simple. It lacked romance. And while Mr. Right hadn't come into her life as yet, she still had hopes.

"What about love?"

"Ridiculous," he scoffed. "What woman wouldn't trade dirty diapers and a crabgrass lawn for a rich and eligible bachelor who could give her a life of wealthy bliss?" He ended the conversation with characteristic aplomb. "The trouble with you, Holly, is that you've lived in Minneapolis too long."

With that, he opened a closet, dragged out a carton, and dumped the contents onto the desk. He flipped a curly brunette wig in her direction. "Here." He stared at her for a moment, then added a pair of mirrored sunglasses.

Yuck. She'd be a brown-haired Little Orphan Annie in that thing! If it didn't get up and walk away first.

"I don't understand," she protested. "Why the disguise? Chadwick doesn't know me."

Digger pointed his finger at her. "For a smart girl, you have no imagination. Chadwick is *your* bachelor. *Yours!* You're to stick to him like glue. For professional reasons only, of course. I once had to fire one of my reporters who got cute and greedy. Don't let me catch you falling for Chadwick!" Apparently satisfied with his warning, Digger continued. "Hang around the apartment house, talk to neighbors—I've already mentioned the garbage—anything else you can think of. Now," he proceeded, getting back to why he wanted her to wear a wig, "suppose Chadwick catches you snooping?"

Holly started to rise. That wasn't what she'd been hired to do. "I don't snoop," she said swiftly. "That's wrong—"

"Oh, for goodness' sake." He came over quickly and pushed her back down in the chair. "We're arguing over semantics. I forgot—this is your first crack at the big time. I should have said *investigative reporting*, your highness. Would that satisfy your misguided notion of morality?"

She wanted to add that sneaking around was wrong whether it was in the so-called "big time" of Hollywood or in the smallest town in America. Values were values; hers had been ingrained since childhood, and she was proud of them.

"I'll figure out a way to get you the information you want in an open and aboveboard manner." She didn't have the foggiest notion of how she'd accomplish the formidable task of making Steven Chadwick do or say anything.

Digger rolled his eyes heavenward, annoyed. "You still need a disguise. While you're figuring out how to uphold your lofty principles, Holly, let me remind you of some cold facts. You might blow it the first time—whatever you dream up. A wig and glasses will let you come back for another go at the man. Then I could still get the information I need for my book. You see my meaning, don't you?"

Clearly. She also saw the wisdom of knowing on which side her bread was buttered, and kept her mouth shut. The rent on her apartment, plus the security deposit and the furniture she had purchased, had drained her bank account. The used Volkswagen she had purchased was on its last legs. For the present, she was stuck playing two ends against the middle.

She sat back and closed her eyes, mentally reliving the good-bye scene at the Minneapolis-St. Paul airport. "Don't worry if you don't succeed in California. Come home—we'll love you regardless." Her parents had excused her failure before it happened.

Regardless stuck in her craw like a fish bone. So did the increasing dissatisfaction with her humdrum existence. Resigned to doing it Digger's way, she opened her eyes.

"What does Chadwick do for a living?" she asked.

"His company builds multiple-unit housing and commercial buildings all over the country. Chadwick's a trained architect and an engineer. Very good too."

Impressive credentials, she agreed. Using the tip of a pencil, she turned her attention back to the wig and lifted her brows in inquiry. "Who wore this?"

A look of pure irritation crossed Digger's thin face. "Nobody. I keep these things in case."

In case of what? "When do I start?"

Digger shifted against the hardness of his chair. "Today. I've arranged for you to use Tom Mason's apartment, which is in Chadwick's building. He owes me a favor. He's away in Europe for six weeks."

She read the scribbled sheet of paper he handed her; she had bad vibes about this. "Are you sure you wouldn't be better handling this yourself?"

"You can hardly expect me to poke into Chadwick's affairs the way a woman can," he replied tartly. "Anyway, I've tried. The man's positively notorious for guarding his privacy. Even Robin failed." Critical gray eyes swept over Holly's blend-into-the-wall outfit. "Believe me, Chadwick'll hardly notice you. You're ideal."

Holly automatically glanced down at her attire; there was nothing unusual. She was wearing a tan skirt, a tan blouse with a nice Peter Pan collar, and sensible, low-heeled tan shoes. She might not be ready for a stroll on Rodeo Drive, but who cared? She dressed for comfort. Holly gritted her teeth, suppressing the ready retort. She'd long since learned it didn't pay to waste her energy on Digger. He was just being his usual unthinking, self-centered self.

She glanced down at the picture on her lap, the unsmiling face pulling at her like a magnet. "What happens if Mason and Chadwick already know one another?"

Digger blithely waved away her concern. "They don't. I checked. Tom moved in a week before leaving on his overseas assignment. It's perfect. Nothing can go wrong."

His answer didn't reassure her. Holly could think of plenty of things that could go wrong!

A few hours later she was craning her neck to get a better view of the Wilshire Boulevard high rise, set among other exclusive buildings in the prime real estate area in Beverly Hills known as Wilshire Gulch. Shining glass windows reflected a panorama of sky and clouds.

Wearing the hateful wig, and feeling like a motorcycle groupie hiding behind the ridiculous mirrored shades, Holly entered the opulent, cool building lobby and strode past a man-made waterfall surrounded by a lush garden of bird-of-paradise and geraniums. She headed straight for the elevator. Her arms were laden with a heavy bag of books, and the rest of her things were still in her red Volkswagen, parked in front of the building between a Mercedes and a Lamborghini.

A tall, broad-shouldered man stood in front of the elevator. He rocked back and forth on his heels, then stopped and stood stiffly erect. Dark brown hair curled low on the collar of a white-on-white tapered shirt that hugged his athletic frame like a second skin and disappeared inside a pair of trim, blue slacks. He held a blue sport jacket in the crook of his arm, and dangled a brown leather attaché case in the other hand. As she coughed, the man turned, a deep frown etching his forehead. His gaze flicked over her briefly; he nodded curtly, barely acknowledging her presence.

Holly's stomach dropped to her knees. The man she'd been admiring—and who exuded an intense aura of virility—was none other than Steven William Chadwick!

The minute the elevator's door slid open, he bolted to the rear. "What floor?" he asked, briskly stepping forward as soon as she had entered the car.

"Twelve," she rasped, noticing for the first time a small, intriguing scar leading away from the right side of his mouth. The picture she'd seen of him had been retouched. It would make wonderful copy if she could find out how he'd acquired it.

He punched twelve and fourteen, then resumed his open-legged stance at the rear wall. Knowing she was protected by her glasses, she slid her eyes up to study his face. His hair was a deeper shade of brown than his picture. Unlike the picture, it wasn't neatly combed, but had a windblown look. His eyes were the color of the wildflower plant she loved so much, and which grew in the fields at home—bachelor-button blue. His nose was marred by a slight bump, another imperfection retouched in his picture. Dark brows formed an arch over thick, spiky lashes. His mouth was firm, with strong, sensuous lips. When he angled his head up, thrusting his jaw forward to focus on the fan of lights above the door, she noticed a very slight twitching of his lips.

Holly loved to read spy novels for relaxation. There were common principles or rules woven through each of the many plots. Spy rule number one: Don't let the person you're following catch you watching him. Could he tell she was memorizing every detail of his face? Spy rule number two: Don't call undue attention to yourself.

Both rules flew out the window as she was attacked by another prodigious coughing and sneezing fit. Tucking her chin over the tip of the bag to release one of her hands, she tried unsuccessfully to reach into her pocket for a tissue.

A clean, white handkerchief materialized under her nose. Embarrassed but grateful, she started to thank her companion for his kindness—until she saw he was eyeing her with an expression somewhat akin to being near a person in the final stages of the bubonic plague. She backed away, but his hand jabbed outward.

"Here. Use this before you give me whatever it is you have," he said insolently.

She stared at the handkerchief and then at him. There was a moment of tense silence while each measured the other's will. She batted away his hand. "I don't take gifts from strangers."

He glowered at her. Unceremoniously, he shoved the linen cloth between her fingers. "It's not an engagement ring, for goodness' sake. Take it!"

She sneezed and grabbed at the same time.

There was no time to prepare for what happened next. The elevator shook violently, then there was a hard, grinding sound, followed in seconds by a jarring halt. Holly was thrown off-balance, and the bag of heavy books dropped onto her foot. She yelped in pain and tried to grab her ankle. Chadwick uttered a loud oath. Suddenly they were on the move again. She felt herself catapulted through space as the elevator shuddered to a stop; she crashed with a shrieking thud against a hard chest, knocking the air out of her companion's lungs. He reacted instinctively by locking her in a viselike grip.

"What happened?" she cried desperately.

"It seems we're stuck," he answered in a thoroughly disgusted tone as he tried to disentangle himself.

As soon as he had pronounced their fate, Holly lunged closer, burrowing herself in the only safety she could find.

Steven Chadwick's warm chest.

She held on to him with a tenacious ferocity. A childhood experience of being locked in an abandoned refrigerator had left her truly frightened of being confined in small spaces. Her hands snaked up to his neck, and she grabbed the soft flesh in a deathlike stranglehold.

A strange, gurgling sound near her ear began to terrify her as much as did her brass-enclosed coffin. She licked her dry lips, forming the words in the hollow of his neck.

"Are we going to die?"

He pried her fingers away from his closed air passage. "Lady," he responded on a choked gasp of air, "I assure you that the only one around here in danger of imminent death is I. Is it necessary to strangle me?" None too gently, he set her away from him, then pushed past her to jab the emergency button. "Damn this thing. I told them it was acting funny."

That was all she had to hear; the blood drained out of her veins, and alarm flared in her eyes. Because of Digger and this—this impolite man, she was sealed up tight in a dangerous elevator.

"I do not want to be here," she announced.

"What makes you think I do?" he snapped.

"Can't you do something?" she demanded.

"Exactly what do you have in mind?"

She jabbed a finger toward the ceiling. "Climb up and open the hatch," she suggested frantically. The tiny square was held in place by four screws.

"Fine," he said. He calmly stepped over the books strewn around the floor and held out his hand to her, as if he were about to ask her to dance.

Confused, she asked, "What's that for?"

He loomed over her. At well over six feet, he filled a good portion of the small interior. "Well," he said implacably, "I can hardly stand on your shoulders and reach the hatch if you don't help."

His composure infuriated her. She glared at him scathingly and immediately became more incensed when he didn't take her seriously. "Very funny. You bend down, I'll stand on you."

His jaw sagged in astonishment. "You're serious, aren't you?" he asked, his voice harsh with surprise.

Her small brows raised in disbelief. "Of course I am. Do you think I'm going to stay here to wait for this can to heat up?"

Steven Chadwick stared at the woman in front of him; she was clearly nuts. Why, of all people, did he have to be stuck with her? If he refused, she'd probably throw her books at him. It seemed better to humor her.

"You're crazy, but we'll try it." He bent down on all fours.

Holly's foot was killing her, but she bravely climbed onto his back, grinding her heel into a tender spot. He uttered a curse as she tried to secure her footing.

"It won't work," she said despondently. "I'm too short."

From below, she heard his disgruntled complaint. "I could have told you it wouldn't work *before* you attempted this circus performance."

She lowered her arms and her body, carefully grabbing his shoulders. Her knees dug into his spine.

"Ouch, dammit! Hurry up," he hissed. "You're no lightweight."

"A gentlemen wouldn't say that!"

"This is hardly the moment to worry about propriety." He got up and arched his back. There were dirt marks from her shoes on his white shirt.

"Maybe I should stand on your shoulders?" she offered hopefully.

He shook his head. "Since neither one of us is a midget, the idea stinks—it was dumb to begin with. Suppose we do get the hatch open, then what? Do you have a bottle of shrinking pills hidden in your purse?"

Behind the mirrored glasses, her eyes flashed. It was true. The most they could get through the tiny opening would be a hand. Since she needed him, she strove to keep her tone reasonable. "Do you have a better idea?"

"As a matter of fact, I do. I suggest that, instead of getting hysterical, you get hold of yourself. There are all sorts of safeguards built into this system."

"Find one," she challenged.

"I'm going to press the emergency button again."

He did. Nothing happened. He swore and picked up the phone inside the elevator. Just his luck—the line was dead.

"We'll have to wait," he announced.

"For how long?" she pressed.

"How the hell do I know? The best thing to do is concentrate on something else." With that, he took his own advice and moved to the other side of the elevator. As far away from her as possible.

But Holly had a one-track mind. "You can tell me the truth. We're going to use up all our oxygen, aren't we?"

"Don't be ridiculous," he said firmly. "We've got plenty of time." Her sharp intake of breath made him regret his poor choice of words. "What I mean is—we'll probably be out of here in no time." The last thing he needed at the moment was an un-glued female.

For the first time Steven Chadwick critically observed the frightened young woman who hid behind an oversized pair of mirrored sunglasses. She wasn't a fashion plate—far from it. Under ordinary circumstances, he wouldn't have paid much attention to her, but this was far from an ordinary circumstance. If she hadn't landed in his arms, he'd never have been able to tell there were any womanly curves or soft breasts beneath the nondescript outfit she wore.

He rubbed his chest. Judging from the way she'd landed against him, and where his head fit atop her brunette curls, he figured her height to be somewhere around five feet four inches tall. She didn't weigh much, but in a tug-of-war, he'd want her playing on his side. She sure could hold on for dear life.

Frankly, he couldn't wait to see the end of this day. The old saying about things going from bad to worse was certainly true, he thought morosely. First, his doctor had warned him he was heading for an ulcer and told him to cut down on stress and change his diet. Second, he'd lost the best cleaning woman he'd ever had. Third, and by far the worst, the housing units his company was building in the north end of Santos had been halted by a building moratorium. The facts were still unclear; all he had been told was that the city had filed a "friendly" lawsuit in superior court to determine if he and other builders could continue building despite the moratorium. In addition to his company, thirty-three other developers stood to lose a fortune while the moratorium remained in force for eighteen months, giving the city time to revise its twenty-three-year-old general plan in compliance with state law. Which, given the fact he'd already had the go-ahead, was a little like putting the cart before the horse.

All the expensive preliminary work had been done: planning commission testimony, documentation, loan approval, demolition, grading, and building permits. Construction crews had been hired; they'd had to cease operation after they'd already broken ground.

And now, to top it off, the young lady with the trembling lower lip gave every indication of going off the deep end if he didn't come up with a way to get her mind off their dilemma.

"I think you'd better sit down and take the pressure off your ankle."

Holly tried, but her clumsy attempt failed, causing her to wince in pain.

With a shake of his head, he wrapped his hands around her arms, pulling her upright against him. He caught a whiff of jasmine. "You're only making things worse."

She didn't care for his dictatorial tone, nor the way he moved, fast as lightning, and tucked his hand below her buttocks. He all but plopped her down onto the floor. As far as she was concerned, both he and Digger could take a flying leap. Only one thing was worse than being stuck in an elevator. She should be home in bed in her nice, safe, first-floor apartment, instead of playing Hercule Poirot for a bunch of love-starved females.

Huddled against the wall, her arms drawn around her knees, she watched him suspiciously while he fiddled at the control panel with a small knife on his key ring. "Now what are you doing?"

"Trying to get us out of here," he replied over his shoulder. "Maybe my Boy Scout training will come in handy."

Struggling to quell her fear, she pressed her thumbs against her throbbing temples. After a moment she simply gave up, and again asked the question uppermost in her thoughts. "How long can the oxygen last?"

Unsuccessful, he put the penknife back on his key chain and turned around. "Long enough. What's your name?"

"Elizabeth Mason," she mumbled. She blurted out her middle name, appropriating her unknown host's surname.

"I'm Steve Chadwick." He softened his tone and leaned against the wall. "Why are you so afraid of elevators, Liz?"

"Elizabeth," she quickly corrected. "I was locked in a refrigerator when I was a child." Her hands played with the folds in her skirt.

Good Lord! No wonder she's been acting like

this. He could hardly blame her. Steve felt a rush of genuine sympathy for her. He also knew that if they weren't rescued soon, he'd have his hands full.

He leveled his gaze at her. *Get her mind off the immediate problem.* "You look like a Liz."

"Exactly what is *that* supposed to mean?" she huffed.

Her frosty reaction produced the desired result. At least now the petrified young woman's mind was focused on something else. He didn't have the faintest idea how long it would be before they'd get out of there.

"Don't take it so personally," he countered, glad he'd hit upon a way to redirect her thoughts. "Liz is a perfectly good name—"

"For a car," she groused, recalling the fourth-grade class buffoon, Charlie Penn, who used to taunt, "Oh, Liz, Tin Liz, Tin Lizzie. You're an old-fashioned car." It had started a rumble among the boys. He had made her nine-year-old life miserable for months, until one day her older brother Mark found out and knocked the bully flat on his back.

Sighing deeply, she mopped the beads of perspiration from her brow. "If you're trying to get me to think of something other than being sealed up in a vertical sardine can, it won't work. Why don't you try the buttons again? Maybe we're near a floor and we can jump."

He doubted it, but he did as she asked. The elevator door opened.

A fresh rattle of panic went through Holly when

she saw an unpainted cement-block wall. Frantically, she squeezed her eyes shut to blot out the sides of her tomb.

"Close it," she whispered timorously.

In an instant, he hunkered down on his knees in front of her. He grasped her clammy hands, kneading them vigorously between his palms. "It might help," he advised, "if we tried to put our minds on something other than our temporary predicament." When she looked at him with doubtful eyes, he slipped down beside her, drawing her quaking, slender form to him.

"What about my cold?" She was at the edge of hysteria.

The smile reached his eyes. He tightened his arms around her. "I'll pop a few extra vitamin Cs when I get home. Now, will you please take off those sunglasses? You have no idea how difficult it is to play a knight rescuing a damsel in distress when I can't see the damsel. All I can see through those mirrors you're wearing is me talking to me. It gives me the weird feeling I've had a sex-change operation and didn't know it."

Even in her fractured state of mind, Holly knew without a doubt that Steven William Chadwick was all male. He smelled of spicy cologne. His five-o'clock shadow was the evidence of a day's growth, and he could have used a shave. Not that she was complaining; if she was going to die, this was not too bad a way to do it.

She made no objection when he removed the glasses from her face. He stared at her for so long she wondered if her wig had slipped. Then he smiled, and the heat inside her had nothing to do with the rising temperature in the elevator. Her heart did a nose dive . . . the first time it ever had. Even Tommy Brighton, the boy she'd dated all through high school and into college, had never made her feel like this.

A warning bell flashed in her mind. *Watch it, Holly. Remember the rules. Don't get personally involved.*

He gently moved a wisp of brunette hair from the corner of her lip and tilted his head. "There, that's better. Those glasses hide your pretty eyes."

She knew he was humoring her—her eyes were puffy—but at a time like this, it felt good. "I'm sorry I made such a fuss," she apologized, setting her affairs in order. "And I'm truly sorry I'm giving you all my germs."

He chuckled. "Considering everything else that's happened to me today, it's par for the course."

Her professional interest was piqued for a moment. "Would you care to tell me about it?"

"Not really," he said.

She nodded her head understandingly. He clearly cherished his privacy. She was quiet for a while; then her thoughts drifted to more important matters. "Oh, dear," she said sadly.

"What's the matter, Liz?" She didn't protest as he crooned the nickname she had hated so much but, on his lips, could grow to adore. Nor did she protest when he extracted a tissue from her open purse and wiped her eyes.

"Nothing," she said in a shaky voice. "I was

thinking I've never made out a will. Do you happen to have a pencil and paper I could borrow, please?"

"You're kidding!" he exclaimed, but he saw immediately she was deadly serious. With some effort, he pulled his lips into a straight line.

She dropped her chin to her chest and snuggled comfortably in his arms, idly playing with the back of his hand. "No. I kept putting it off. I'm usually so healthy—you can't count this cold."

Above her, he murmured, "Of course not."

She bobbed her head. "I thought I had plenty of time. I'm still so young. Twenty-four's not old, is it?"

"Hardly." He lost the battle with his lips.

"It just proves the old adage, or proverb, or whatever it is . . ."

"What's that, Liz?" he asked in all seriousness. He was glad she couldn't see his face.

She wrung her hands. "You should never put off for tomorrow what you can do today. Isn't that so?"

"Definitely." He patted her arm.

Sighing, she patted his in return. She forgave him for being such a stinker before. When the chips were down, he'd come through admirably. She dripped large teardrops as she went on sincerely. "I always meant to write letters to the people who mean the most to me."

"That's certainly wise. Keeping in touch, I mean."

"And then there's Oscar."

He glanced at her ringless finger. "Is Oscar your husband?" She shook her head. "Your boyfriend?"

"My dog," she said matter-of-factly. Oscar was home in Minneapolis. Enjoying the lilacs, no doubt.

"Liz." Her protector stopped trying to contain himself and burst out laughing. "Don't be a silly goose. You don't have to draw up a will just yet. The men are working on this ungodly space shuttle right now. I can hear them. Shhh. Listen." The voices grew louder. "We'll be out of here in no time."

"Do you really think we will?" she asked tentatively.

He held up his hand. "Cross my heart and hope to—"

She placed her fingers to his lips. "If you don't mind, don't finish that, please."

He just laughed and shook his head. Her pale little face looked up at him so trustingly. "Come here." He pulled her back into the protective circle of his arms. The most delicious sensations rippled through her, reaching every nerve in her body. For the next few moments, she wondered quietly how something that had started out so terrifyingly could end up feeling so good.

He shifted her off his lap, careful to continue to support her side until she sat upright on her own.

"What are you doing?" she asked huskily.

He moved his fingertips to her ankle, pressing it so lightly it could have been a butterfly's kiss. "Just checking for breaks. Do you mind?" He lifted his eyes for permission, and Holly could have drowned in their blue depths.

He added gentle pressure with the pads of his

fingers. "I think," he assured her, "it's nothing more than a sprain."

Mesmerized, she watched his hand go up her leg—manipulating and putting pressure on her calf. He rubbed the skin where needles and pins had begun; under his tender ministrations, the circulation returned.

She gazed at his dark head as he bent, so intent on his labors. She was fascinated by his hands, and watched his long, steady strokes, wondering how those knowledgeable hands would feel if they were traveling over the length of her body. Thinking about it made her nipples harden.

At that moment his hands traveled higher, reaching the sensitive underpart of her knee. She pulled back, sucking in air on a gasp of breath.

He glanced up quickly. "Did I hurt you?"

Holly shook her head. She didn't trust herself to speak. He would never hurt her—his touch was too gentle, his manner too kind.

"What kind of work do you do?" he asked, returning to her side.

His eyes were so compelling, so tranquilly innocent. Remember the rules: Don't get suckered in by a pair of drop-dead blue eyes.

"Research," she said truthfully. "I gather background information for large companies, authors, anyone who needs facts or historical records but doesn't have the time to spare to gather them personally."

He seemed genuinely interested. He started to ask another question, but she blocked it with one she already knew the answer to. "What do you do?"

"I'm an architect. My company builds in various parts of the country. Does your throat hurt much? It sounds awful."

"Actually, it's killing me. It's much easier if you do the talking." She blessed the gods for the opening; she wasn't ready to talk about herself. She hadn't figured out yet how she would interview him, only knowing now wasn't the time.

Voices shouted down to them that they'd be out in a jiffy. There was no time for further discussion. With a feeling of regret, she realized she'd missed a golden opportunity.

"We're ready," someone called. "It may be a little bumpy, but we'll have you out of there in no time."

True to their word, the repairmen had the elevator back in service within minutes. The door slid open on Holly's floor and she turned to Steven. Now that the misadventure was clearly over, she experienced an inexplicable sense of loss. For a short while, they had been the most intimate of friends; now the moment of intimacy had passed. They were strangers again. Worse—she had a job to do which would end their friendship. Feeling like a cheat, she extended her hand.

His eyes swept over her flustered face. "What's that for?"

She started to speak but was forced to clear her throat. This wasn't going to be easy. Not with those clear, innocent, blue eyes staring at her.

"I—I want to thank you for all you've done for me. I know it was difficult having an hysterical female on your hands."

He surveyed her with tender amusement, a glint in his eye. Nodding his head gravely, he added, "Especially an hysterical female who's injured and might have a fever."

He bent down to hand her the repacked bag of books. As soon as it was deposited in her arms, she was scooped up in his.

"What—what are you doing?" she stammered, curbing the impulse to run her fingers through his hair.

"Taking you home. Do you have a problem with that?"

Two

Why didn't she insist he leave her at "her" door? Why didn't she protest when he didn't say goodbye? The answer, she knew, had something to do with the fact that there was an explosion of heat coming from the pit of her stomach. Still, it was risky business, letting him in when she didn't have the foggiest notion about the apartment's floor plan. But all of James Bond's bag of tricks couldn't have made her open her mouth. Nothing like this had ever happened to her.

Her life was so ordered, so mundanely routine she was ready to scream. She was tired of hunting through musty old files, tired of preparing questionnaires, tired of tabulating results. Tired of writing scholarly reports. Tired of smiling gaily into the camera at all her friends' weddings!

Mostly she was just tired of letting life pass her by.

"Go west, young man." In this case, she had adapted the advice given by Horatio Alger to suit her own purpose. Rotten as the terrifying interlude in the elevator was, in retrospect, it certainly was worth meeting Steven Chadwick.

Digger would probably give her a bonus for being able to furnish a firsthand impression of what it felt like to have a rich and famous bachelor carry you across the threshold. Even if her knight carefully kept his face averted so as not to catch her cold. A girl can dream.

She could feel the strength of his body as he carried her effortlessly down the wide hall. At number fifteen, he dipped his powerful frame so she could turn the key in the lock; then he nudged the door open with his shoulder. Anxious to catch a glimpse of her new living quarters, she craned her neck for a first view. And what a breathtaking view it was!

For starters, she swiftly noted, the tiled entryway and spacious room flowing beyond it were larger than her entire North Hollywood studio apartment. The enormous living room was decorated almost exclusively in white, from the oversized leather sofa and conversation area to the baby grand piano to the Italian marble fireplace that rose majestically to the cathedral ceiling. She did a quick mental calculation of the room. Seven-hundred-fifty square feet.

"Nice," he commented, checking the view of Wilshire Boulevard after depositing her gently on the sofa.

Yes, you are, she thought, easily distracted by

his broad shoulders. She propped her foot up on a pillow. "Is your apartment this large?"

"A bit larger." He inspected a Baccarat crystal bowl on a burnished cherry wood side table.

A bit larger! She had been told his family had settled in California when the priests first traveled the El Camino Real. Tomorrow she would go to the office and read everything about him and his family she could get her hands on.

Lifestyles were just a question of degree. She had lived in one house her entire life. On Portland Avenue in the Diamond Lake area of Minneapolis, the two-story clapboard her parents had purchased thirty years ago had a wraparound porch, blue wicker furniture, and creaky front steps. Oscar guarded the property by yawning loudly if strangers came.

It was a happy home. Her parents had struggled to give their children the best education they could afford; both she and her brother Mark had held after-school jobs to help. Mark had majored in law, while she pursued the unlikely combination of English literature and nutrition.

She relaxed, watching Steven stroll over to peer first at a Jasper Johns lithograph and pause longer to study a still life painting depicting summer fruits. The later hung above a banquette upholstered in a silk striped fabric of raspberry, plum, and beige.

"Peacocks run wild on my property," he said, stopping at a Chinese urn filled with the brilliant plumage of peacock feathers.

This was the first piece of information he had

offered about himself. She was instantly alert. "Where is that?"

"Palos Verdes."

"Is that where you grew up?" Later she would transcribe the information into notes.

"There, and other places." He moved on to a side cabinet filled with miniature antiques; he seemed particularly interested in a jeweled egg. "Fabergé," he commented, recognizing the work of the renowned artist to the Czar of Russia.

He came back to loom over her, studying her for a moment. Her heart reacted by doing flip-flops every time he came near her.

He checked his wristwatch. "Are you going to be all right? Is there anything you need before I leave? You look kind of beat."

She would never be all right again, but she'd have to deal with that. All the men in her life thus far couldn't hold a candle to him—not in the looks department or in the way he made her feel. And the pity of it was, she looked like hell. No wonder he was ready to bolt.

She threw him a martyred look. "Of course I'm going to be okay."

He picked up his attaché case and jacket. His hand was on the doorknob when he hesitated, his forehead wrinkling in consternation. "Your ankle needs an ice pack."

He was right—it *did* need ice. It throbbed like hell, and the swelling hadn't gone down; the flesh had turned a punky purple. He tossed his jacket and case back onto the chair. Imagining how she must appear, she had never felt uglier or puffier in her life.

"Don't bother. I'll get it when you leave."

"No," he forcefully disagreed. "I should have thought of it immediately. Pressure is the one thing you don't need. I'm curious about something. Aside from elevators, are you always getting yourself into trouble?"

She smiled, remembering all the scrapes she had gotten into with her brother. "The truth, or what sounds good?"

He chuckled. "Figures."

"What's that supposed to mean?"

"Something tells me, Liz Mason, you need a guardian."

Her pulse speeded up to a dangerous level. She took a reckless chance. "Are you applying for the job?"

He looked at her as if she'd given him a choice between two evils—bad news and worse news. "Hardly. I'm trying to get you off my conscience."

All her kind thoughts about him flew out the window. While she was unwisely mixing business with pleasure, and falling for him like a ton of bricks, he was confessing he hated being saddled with an unwanted burden—her!

"Go home," she huffed, disgusted with herself for asking a leading question. "You're off-duty. I'm quite capable of getting my own ice pack, thank you."

He sat down on a club chair and stretched his long legs out in front of him. He folded his hands across his lap. And twiddled his thumbs.

"Prove it. If you can walk, so will I—I'll leave."

Holly wanted to bounce up and wipe the smug

look off his face. Glaring at him, she pushed herself up to a sitting position. Then she stood up. But she did it without thinking. The pain exploded behind her eyes and she grabbed the side of the couch.

He flew out of the chair. "You little fool," he said, helping her to lie back down on the couch. Beads of perspiration dotted her upper lip. She closed her eyes and gritted her teeth.

"All right, Liz! Now we'll try it my way." She opened her eyes to see him disappear from view.

She waited for the sharp ache in her foot to subside. It did so sooner than her embarrassment. She wasn't the type to throw herself at men, however teasingly *or* innocently. Yet Steven Chadwick had her doing things totally out of character.

She heard him prowling around the kitchen. When he returned with ice cubes wrapped in a towel, there was a look of total disapproval on his face. His eyes blazed furiously into hers. The late rays of the sun streamed through the windows, backlighting his hair like a fiery god's.

"When's the last time you went shopping?" he demanded, shoving the ice pack into her hand. "The only thing in the fridge is catsup, mayonnaise, and a jar of pickles that look as if they're growing hair. I thought *I* didn't know anything about nutrition, but you take the cake!" He hitched a shoulder in the direction of the still life. "Do you realize there's more food in that painting than there is in this house?"

Holly stared at him in speechless wonder. Her

eyebrows lifted above the tortoiseshell glasses she'd donned. *Why—he's worried about me!* she realized, happily putting him back into her good graces. Why else would he be so gorgeously disgruntled?

She quickly forgave his flare-up and his snide remark about her culinary abilities. She almost blurted out that she was an excellent cook; she'd always been known for her creative dishes. In fact, she was compiling a list of her tried and true recipes to write a cookbook when she found the time. Someday, if she got the chance, she'd prepare him a gourmet dinner.

"The empty refrigerator's not my fault," she said, giving him a praline-sugar smile. She also gave herself an instant family on the West Coast as she tested her sudden brainstorm.

"I'm apartment-sitting for my cousin. Tom—he's my cousin—Tom's afraid a burglar would be attracted to an empty apartment."

She watched as he digested the news. The muscles on his face hadn't changed one iota. His voice was deceptively innocent.

"Then who's in your apartment, guarding it from crooks, while you're here guarding this place from crooks?"

"No one," she sighed, and demurely lowered her lashes. This man was a certified slippery eel! It was time for Sarah Bernhardt to take center stage. "I'm taking my chances, I know." She opened her palms in a gesture of giving. "When I was coming up before, I was carrying my first load of things."

She sincerely hoped he'd get the message.

He looked at his watch. "I'll get the rest of your things in a minute. Right now, I don't suppose you know where your cousin keeps a pencil and paper, do you?" he asked, confirming her guess that he was at the end of his tether.

She sighed deeply. "Sorry."

He rose abruptly. Extracting a pad and gold pencil from his case, he came back and sat down on the couch. "I'm ready," he said without preamble. He leaned forward, and Holly inhaled the spicy, male scent of cologne. To her great disgust, he was treating her in much the same way her older brother Mark did when they were kids and she had been ill.

Impatient and out of sorts.

He tapped the pencil on the pad resting on his lap. "Listen," he said sternly, "I'm going to order in some food for myself *and* for you. From what I can see, you need a lot of protection. Mostly from yourself."

"I'll be fine," she protested, adding a wince for punctuation.

He peered at her from beneath a ridge of dark brows. "I can see that."

She favored him with a weak, theatrical smile. "This isn't India. You're not responsible for me."

He threaded his fingers through his hair. When he spoke, it was more in wonder at his own thoughts than in answer to her question. "Then tell me why I'd have a guilty conscience if I just left you laying on the couch to fend for yourself?"

She saw an opening and grabbed it. If she played her cards right, she'd have her interview all tied up in a neat package.

"It probably has something to do with your childhood training. Do you like women?"

"There was a silence of disbelief. *Was she asking if he was a homosexual?* His eyes slid to hers. "I love women."

Good. She congratulated her foresight; she was making headway. "A lot, or is there one special woman?"

"That's none of your business," he said, flatly exasperated.

She made a tactical retreat, flinging her arm up over her eyes. "I've taken up enough of your time."

"Oh, for goodness' sake." He snatched her hand away from her face. "I didn't mean to snap at you," he snapped. "I'll be glad to stay and help you," he offered angrily. "You ought to take a few days off from your work, anyway." He began to make out the list.

"What are you writing down? I haven't said anything yet."

He finished his pre-list. "I'm going to fix you a guggle muggle."

"A what?" she asked in horrified tones.

"A guggle muggle."

She made a terrible face. "It sounds like a disease."

"It's a sure cure for what ails you."

"What's in it?" She didn't trust anything with a name like that.

He sloughed over the ingredients. "Hot milk, butter, honey, and rum."

She gagged. "No, thank you."

He put the pencil down for a moment. His tone was persuasive. "I grew up on them. Believe me, I rarely was sick."

"I can see why," she said irascibly. "It was self-defense."

He bit his lip to keep from laughing at her perception; she had come awfully close to the truth. He stared at her flushed face. She looked so damned earnest, fighting him like a little kid. He had to remind himself she was a grown woman with a respectable job. To steer her mind in a different direction, he asked, "By the way, what exactly are you researching now?"

"Now?" she stammered. This would be a perfect time for a sneeze, she thought, searching for a way to avoid his penetrating gaze. Where was it when she needed it?

A dark lock of his hair had fallen down on his forehead, his tie was loosened from its knot, and the top button of his shirt was open. He looked marvelous, masculine, and sexy. And waiting for an answer.

She shifted uncomfortably, thankful he assumed her distress was caused by her throbbing ankle.

"Now," he echoed, adjusting the ice pack for her.

"Movie stars of yesteryear. I find out what's happened to them over the years. I track them down, find out where they're living, and—whenever I can—I interview them."

She couldn't have chosen a worse subject short of admitting the truth: that she was now "working" on him, but didn't think he was in the mood to give an in-depth interview.

Like an exuberant kid, he became revitalized. His eyes sparkled. While she lay there, stunned by the change in him, he launched into a lengthy list of stars he wanted her to find out about. As he gestured, the order pad slipped to the floor. He was, she learned to her horrified dismay, a confirmed, dyed-in-the-wool movie buff.

"Especially Lance Trainor," he said, his face wreathed in a smile at fond memories. "I used to sit through his westerns until my eyes popped. In fact," he added excitedly, "if you find him, I'll go with you when you interview him."

"I've never heard of him," she replied hastily.

He brightened. "You haven't lived until you've seen one of his pictures. I'll rent one of his movies from the video store and run it for you. If they haven't been transcribed for VCRs, I'll see what I can do about borrowing one from the studio."

"You can do that?"

"Of course. I have connections."

"Doesn't everybody?" she murmured.

"What do you mean by that?" he asked.

"Nothing. Nothing at all. I don't even know what prompted me to say it." Now what would happen if Digger's connections bumped into Steven's connections? *That* should make for an interesting turn of events.

As she talked, his hand dropped down to casually rest on her knee. The contact was shooting sparks up her thigh. Holly was uncomfortably aware of the fact that, even without conscious effort on his part, he could make her blood race.

"What else have you researched?"

"*Helped* research," she corrected. Thinking back to her student days, she said, "One of the most interesting projects I worked on was body-watching."

"Body-watching. I like that," he said enthusiastically. "I didn't know you had to be a scientist to do that. Neither," he chuckled at his own humor, "do the rest of the guys I know."

"For your information, smartie, there's quite a lot to be learned from watching bodies!"

"Oh, I agree." He pulled back in time to escape the pillow she threw at him. "Sorry," he apologized, not sounding sorry one bit. "Go on, please."

"Take, for instance, the nose." He looked disappointed, and she hastened to continue. "I bet you don't know why many people who live in very hot climates, like the desert, have noses that protrude more than people who live in cooler places," she asked smugly.

He shook his head. He had never thought it important. On a scale of one to ten, he gave it a minus one.

"It's because the nose is an air conditioner. Over time, the nose developed to accommodate the drawing in of air."

"Marvelous."

"It also heats up during sex," she said, and was immediately rewarded with a lecherous look in his eye.

"Now *that* I want to hear."

She stopped, embarrassed. "Let's get on with the order," she said huskily.

"Oh, no. I never realized how sorely my education was lacking. You started this, and now you have my undivided attention. Why does the nose heat up during sex?"

She rushed through her explanation as quickly as possible. "It has something to do with glands and hormones. The entire face heats up, including the ears. The . . . um, uh . . . isn't the only thing to heat up during tumescence." Let him figure out the missing word. If this kept up, she'd be a basket case.

"You know that for a fact, do you?" he asked, straight-faced.

"I . . . I'm only quoting the facts," she sputtered.

"What else do you know—about body-watching, I mean?"

Why had she opened her big mouth? "Well, there's always the theory about the origin of kissing."

"Is there now?" He smiled broadly. "Go ahead. I can't wait."

"It has to do with baby food." He raised a dubious brow. "We really don't know how many years ago it started, but the theory is that mothers, like birds, had to feed their young food that the baby could swallow. Don't forget, babies can't masticate, and there was no baby food or markets. You *do* know what mother birds do, don't you?"

He drew back. "Naturally. They chew the food up and transfer it into the tiny baby's mouth. What does that have to do with kissing?"

"The action of transferring food with lips—human lips—and making skin contact, was seen as an act of love. Minus the food . . . it's kissing!"

"Amazing! What else do you know?"

She blushed. "There's always the breast."

"My favorite part."

So her big mouth had led her to another piece of information about Steven Chadwick. Thinking about that, she answered him clinically. "The human species is the only one where the female retains the shape of the breast in periods of nonlactation."

"Amen to that," he said seriously.

She swatted his hand. "You're terrible. Here I am, giving you valuable information—which you asked for—and you're making fun."

"Liz, stop sounding like a college professor. Can I help it if I want to think of the female body as something more romantic than a scientific lecture on *Homo sapiens*, female variety."

"I suppose you think an evening with a beautiful movie star is more informative?" she huffed.

"I certainly do," he agreed heartily. "Now, let's get on with the list."

She didn't want any part of the list; she already knew what was on it. "I'll buy some tea, and we can forget about the guggle muggle."

Dr. Chadwick answered much the same as a scowling Ben Casey. "No."

She knew she was fighting a losing battle, but she was still protesting loudly as he rose and left her to get the phone number of the neighborhood store.

"I've taken up enough of your time," she called, really meaning it this time. "After you leave, I'll take a bath, make some tea, and hop into bed."

He popped his head back into the room through the open doorway and pointed to her swollen ankle propped up on the pillow. "Hop? Into what? The bathtub? You've already proven you're the walking wounded. By your own admission, this is a new neighborhood for you. You don't know where the stores are—"

"I didn't say that."

"Well, do you?"

"No," she admitted truthfully.

He uttered an exasperated sound. "Just as I said, you need the whole treatment."

"Why are you being so good to me?" she groaned.

He didn't know himself. All he knew was, for some crazy reason, he *did* feel responsible for her. It surprised the life out of him. How, he wondered, could an experience in an elevator with a woman who cried because she wasn't going to outlive a dog get to him? He didn't take time to separate his feelings for her; they were all mixed-up with exasperation, admiration, and humor. She was sick, injured, and spending her first night alone in a strange apartment. So how could he leave her? He convinced himself he would have done the same for anyone.

"You're the one who mentioned the Indian saying," he answered finally. "I saved your life, now I'm responsible."

Her eyes twinkled—he hadn't added the rest of the saying. Save a person's life; he's your responsibility for life. The thought of being in his care for life intrigued her. "We're not in India," she reminded him practically.

"But the principle applies."

"Are you always so bossy?"

"Probably," he commented.

"Well, don't do me any favors. I'm quite used to taking care of myself. How far do you intend to carry this?"

"Until you're safely tucked in bed."

"No way." Before she went to bed, she was going to rip off the wig and scrub her hair until it squeaked. "And no guggle muggle either," she announced, fixing him with a beady-eyed stare.

He grinned. "Wanna bet?"

She was about to argue, but realized that behind his easy stance was a knight prepared to slay anything in his way. No, she'd show him she was able to take care of herself.

She pulled the pillow out from under her foot. She smoothed down her skirt. She gingerly swung her leg off the sofa, touching her foot down onto the carpeting. This time she'd make it; hot milk, honey, butter, and rum was a powerful antidote.

Her knees started to buckle.

"Dammit! Stop being a hero," Steven ordered, swiftly coming to her aid.

"Heroine," she corrected weakly, giving in to the luxury of leaning on him.

"Are you always so obstinate?" He helped her back to the sofa and propped her foot back up in place.

She breathed in short gulps. "When I'm desperate."

He muttered something about her being more trouble than she was worth. She flopped back on a pillow, allowing herself to be pampered. He made two trips to her car to bring up her suitcases, and within half an hour the food was delivered. He disappeared into the kitchen again, only to reappear with a satisfied look on his face and the offensive cure in his hand.

She took one look at the repulsive concoction; no way was she going to get his "cure" past her lips. "You're smiling because you don't have to drink it, aren't you?" she groused.

He crouched down to help her to a sitting position. "Absolutely. It's a feeling of intense power."

"What's with you, anyway?" she stormed in her husky voice. "Don't you know we're living in the twentieth century? I suppose you use leeches too!"

"Don't knock it," he drawled, unaffected by her stinging rebuke. "Leeches have made a respectable comeback in microsurgery, especially brain surgery. A little research on the subject won't hurt you. Now, drink up!"

She glared at him. "I am not going to drink that thing."

Her announcement didn't faze him. "Don't be childish. What will your boss say if I tell him you refused medical help?"

"I'd rather die." Much as she liked him, she wished he would go away. She saw herself being greeted back at the Minneapolis-St. Paul airport by her parents who loved her *regardless*. Why not? She'd already blown her cover. She was stuck in this stupid wig. She'd lied about Tom Mason. Digger would call her an idiot—if he didn't fire her first! The tension was giving her a blasted headache.

She clamped her mouth shut.

"Drink!"

Her hazel eyes were the color of thunderclouds before a storm. "To get rid of you!" She tilted the mug in a mock toast.

"Liz, you're a royal pain in the ass. I should have let you make out the damned will." He checked his watch for the third time. "Damn," he muttered. "I've got to make a phone call before I finish with you. Louise is probably wondering where I am."

Louise?

Her heart sank as Steven dialed the phone. He spoke in low, intimate tones to the woman on the other end of the line. When he hung up, there was a satisfied look of anticipation on his handsome face.

Scratch one bachelor, she thought miserably. *This one's taken.*

Three

Steven let himself into his penthouse suite. He was tired and still steaming mad because of the elevator breakdown. He had chosen this exclusive apartment building because of its proximity to his Century City office. With the freeways the clogged mess they were, and with the California road density becoming an increasing nightmare of frayed nerves, he was able to drive the short distance to work without wasting valuable time. When he was living here, he expected excellent service. On the weekends he usually escaped to his home in Palos Verdes, where he played golf, or his home up the coast near Oxnard, where he kept his forty-five-foot fishing boat.

His mind went back tenaciously to Liz. It was inexcusable to put her through such a harrowing experience. He could well imagine—no—on second thought, he couldn't begin to imagine how frightening it must have been for her as a young child to be locked inside a refrigerator. If he could get his hands on whoever had played such a rotten prank on her, he'd break his damned neck.

She *was* a feisty one. She fought him down to the wire over the guggle muggle—not that he blamed her. It wasn't until he'd threatened to swab her chest with a mustard plaster that she'd given in.

Loosening his tie, he walked into the dining room. He smiled a greeting to the stunning redhead setting the candles in the silver candlesticks on the banquet-sized table. The lights on the crystal chandelier were dimmed to an intimate glow. The table, with its salmon-colored Irish linen cloth, was set for twenty people.

"Hi, sorry I'm late. Is Larry here?"

"Not yet." The statuesque beauty with violet eyes strolled over to kiss him. She was dressed in a slinky, violet silk gown. Her hair was piled on top of her head, showing off her latest acquisition. Three carat diamond drop earrings.

"Nice." He touched the white fire. "Larry?"

She shook her head. "No, me. You know he's into basics. The last thing he bought me was a toaster oven. Can you imagine? I brought it to his place—he didn't have one. I think he's trying to tell me my past indiscretions don't mesh with his old-fashioned notion of a 'Leave-it-to-Beaver' mommy."

Louise Armand was old money and new money and a jet-setter. She and Steve had been friends since childhood. At one time, they'd talked about the fact that it was too bad they hadn't fallen in love. But friendship was all it was, and all it would ever be.

Five years ago during a trip to Rome, she had accepted a movie role, as a lark. Much to her surprise, she had discovered she had both talent as an actress and a penchant for hard work. Her movie credits included one picture with Paul Newman and one with Tom Cruise. She was also madly in love with Steve's best friend Larry Powers, who occupied an apartment in the building.

"I'd give it all up in a moment. Why the hell won't he ask me to marry him, Steve? You're his best friend."

He patted her trim backside. "Which is why I'm letting you throw his little birthday shindig here. I draw the line at asking him why he isn't ready to settle down."

She made a moue with her famous mouth. "You men are all alike. Maybe if you were married, it would give him ideas."

He tossed his silk tie onto a chair. Without picking it up, he headed for his bedroom, which was cluttered with yesterday's clothes. He sat down on a chair. "Not me, thank you. I have no interest in entering the matrimonial state of wedded bliss, where fifty percent of the marriages break up."

Louise leaned against the doorjamb, twirling his tie over her fingers. She waved a celery stick in her other hand, the crimson polish on her nails contrasting with the pale green stalk. "The trouble with you, snookums—"

"Stop calling me that ridiculous name. Save it for Larry."

"The trouble with you, snookums," she continued, ignoring his order, "is you're a cynic. You slither off like a snake every time a woman gets too close."

"I do not," he protested, knowing full well there was a measure of truth in her words. "I just enjoy being a bachelor. Shoot me if that's a cardinal offense."

"You'll have to find three women," Louise went on. "One: A maid to straighten out this mess. It doesn't fit your image. Two: A fabulous cook who'll cater to your ulcer."

"My almost-ulcer," he corrected, dropping his shoe on the floor with a loud thud. "Doc's put me on probation. What's the third?"

She winked. "I'll leave that to you." Tossing her head, she left him alone to change.

He was tired. It had been a long, grueling day. He was worried about business. He wished he could close the door and do what Liz was doing now—sleeping, he hoped.

He fought the urge to call her and see if she was all right. Poor kid. She had been so scared. And so funny. She actually had been serious about making out a will. It didn't surprise him to learn she wasn't one of the tenants in the building, especially after seeing her dented Volkswagen.

He laughed, remembering how she had held her nose to drink the guggle muggle. He had done the same thing when he was a kid. She was smart too. Even though her explanations on body-watching came out funny, she was nobody's fool.

He switched on the playback mode of his answering machine. He made a note to call Larry to contact the Santos Planning Commission chairman; his friend was also his company's chief counsel. If he ever married Louise, it would draw his little family into a tight circle combining friendship, business, and pleasure.

The last message was from his nineteen-year-old sister Ginger. Wondering what scheme she had cooked up this time, he dialed her number. "What do you want, sprite?" he asked as soon as he heard her voice. Today she was imitating Marilyn Monroe.

"I did that pretty good, didn't I? When are you going to be out of town?"

Following her thinking was like following a high-speed train. She always left him feeling his age. "Not really, and I'm not sure. Possibly next weekend. Why?"

"Fran and I want to use your place."

"What do you mean by 'use'?" he asked suspiciously. "Use as in a slumber party? Use as in a place to change your clothes? Use as in make out? What?"

"Gawd, dahling." Ginger did her interpretation of Tallulah Bankhead. "Use as in a place to sleep. Fran and I are invited to a marvelous party in town. You don't want us to sleep at the guys' frat house, do you?"

"Absolutely not! You're much too attractive for your own good, young lady."

She laughed warmly. "Yeah, you're only saying that because you're partial to blondes."

"True, and you're a very special one. It's a dangerous world out there." He knew from past conversations she understood his meaning regarding the sexual climate in the world now and the need for caution.

Ginger switched to her normal voice. "Hey, are you okay? You sound so serious all of a sudden. This isn't a major request for funds, just a flophouse bed for the night."

"You missed your calling, kid. You should be majoring in theater arts at USC instead of psychology." He shook away a vision of Liz balancing her right foot on her left instep. Ginger would have made a major production out of a slight scratch. "It's a major sacrifice, but you girls can use the place whether I'm here or not."

She squealed into the phone. "I knew I could count on you."

"Say hello to Mother for me, pest. It's not easy having a change-of-life baby." He put the receiver back on the cradle and left the slip of paper with Liz's number near the phone.

India. Could it be there *was* something to the expression after all? Whether there was or not, he intended to check on her first thing in the morning.

Holly awoke feeling infinitely better in body, but not in spirit. The problem was, she kept getting blurred images of Steven. Was he really just a bossy, obstinate, dictatorial, conceited, opinion-

ated man whose rich lifestyle and devastingly marvelous good looks let him get away with those
traits? Or was he a tender, considerate, solici-
tous, kind, caring, bossy, obstinate, dictatorial,
conceited, opinionated heartthrob who didn't give
a damn what people thought?

Louise would know! Maybe she should interview her?

Holly stared up at the ceiling. She'd been awake
for an hour. Much as she hated to admit it, Steven's vile drink had done the trick. Her cold had
improved, which meant it was time for work. Bed
is for the idle rich, not the working poor, she
thought, wishing she could loll about. She'd take
it easy, though. She intended to return to the
office and read all about Steven. If that didn't
work, there was always the public library.

What she did know about him was sketchy. He
was a builder who liked cowboy movies—she preferred foreign art films. He liked women with
breasts—hers weren't anything to write home
about. Peacocks roamed on his property. Well,
maybe Digger could make something out of that.
She mentally wrote the copy: *The buxom beauty
who captures this bachelor's interest will no
doubt be attired in her best Annie Oakley original, riding on a peacock.*

Not enough. Not nearly enough.

She sat up, swung her legs over the side of the
massive bed, and cautiously stood up. Her ankle—
although tender—supported her. The flesh around
the bruise had turned a nice, sickly yellowish-green.

Slipping into a pair of blue mules, she padded

into the sumptuous bathroom off the master suite. She showered and washed her hair, enjoying the balming warmth of the jet spray on her sore muscles. Later, clad in a blue dressing gown, she sat in front of a beveled mirror; her long, golden tresses were hidden under a towel she had wrapped turban-style around her head.

During the night she had had a nightmare. Like a miracle, Steven appeared to soothe away the demons. Even now she saw his blue eyes, his well-defined features—she heard his commanding tone so clearly he could have been standing right beside her.

She folded her arms and wrapped them around her stomach, rocking on the hard knot that formed every time she thought about him. *Put things in their proper perspective,* she admonished herself. Sensible people—if nothing else, she was sensible —do not fall in love with someone just because of a simple act of kindness. *The poor man was saddled with you. That's all it was.*

She removed the terry cloth towel and picked up the hair dryer. Her mind was two floors up. She was so consumed by her troubled musings she didn't hear the phone. And when she finally did, she let it ring several more times. She had no desire to speak with Digger.

"Hello," she said dully when she finally picked it up.

She heard a relieved sigh, followed by an angry question. "What took you so long? Are you all right?"

She'd know Steven's impatient tone anywhere.

She willed her pulse to calm down. "Better. I've decided to go to work."

He muttered a nonapproving curse.

"Did you hear me? I said I'm going to work."

"Yes, I heard you. Don't be so stupid. I can still hear your cold. I'm sure your ankle needs a day's rest. Stay off it. Stay home," he commanded.

Before she knew it she was shouting. "No, I will not stay here! I'm leaving in exactly half an hour. Unlike others who reside in this palace, *I* have to make a living."

"That's reverse snobbery and you know it," he charged.

"I'm still going to work."

"Fine!" he snapped. "Have a good day. There's plenty more milk, honey, butter, and rum where that guggle muggle came from. If you need crutches for your foot, I'll be happy to furnish you with the name of a drugstore where you can rent a pair."

"Stop taking this Indian tradition so seriously!" Holly said in annoyance. He cut the connection. *To Louise*, she fumed, *he purrs like a lover. To me, he hisses like an angry cat.*

She ate her breakfast of juice and cereal like a robot. After washing the dishes—and breaking one by mistake—she hobbled into the bedroom to choose what to wear. Her choice was easy; planning on going back to her own place for her mail and more clothing, she had only brought two skirts—tan and navy. She choose the navy, and a crisply starched white cotton blouse with tiny seed pearl buttons. She added a white-and-blue scarf to complete the ensemble.

Then she couldn't get her foot into her shoe.

She could almost hear Steven gloating—*I told you so!* She gave up and slipped her feet into a pair of sandals. Wig in place, she flung her purse over her shoulder and closed the door behind her.

Now she was faced with a new dilemma: How was she going to screw up her courage and get back on that elevator? With slow determination, she psyched herself up. Telling herself all would be well, she forced herself to walk around the corner to test her mettle.

She almost cried with relief. Steven—dressed in fawn-colored slacks, an open-necked, matching sport shirt, and polished brown loafers—was propped against the frame preventing the elevator door from closing.

Her heart did a crazy somersault. *He knows!* That sweet, wonderful man knew she'd be afraid. In spite of everything, he had come to help her. She started to call to him, then realized he wasn't alone. Far from it. His arm was draped possessively around the shoulder of the most gorgeous-looking redhead Holly had ever seen in her life. Their heads were close together, and they were laughing about something.

Steven was the first to look up. Then his companion lifted her head. Holly wanted to vanish into thin air. The woman was even more beautiful close up. There was something familiar about this woman with wide-set Elizabeth Taylor eyes and a regal carriage. No wonder he couldn't wait to get home last night.

Wordlessly, Steven reached his hand across the

sill. He took Holly's small hand reassuringly in his. The reassurance, however, didn't reach his chilly blue eyes. It was clear he thought she should be in bed, resting.

"Good morning." He greeted her civilly, aloofly, as if he hadn't just gotten off the phone from yelling at her. "Liz Mason, Louise Armand. Liz is the woman I told you about."

Louise glanced up, murmured a soft greeting, then resumed her private tête-à-tête with Steven.

Oh, wonderful! Holly thought. *He's told her about me. With all my fears and warts hanging out.* She tried, gracefully, to extract her hand, but each time she did, he clamped his fingers more tightly around it. Finally, she simply gave up. She was the third party—the outcast.

With a sinking heart, she listened to the two chat about their wonderful evening together. When Louse cooed, "I'm sorry about mussing up the bed," Holly closed her eyes. They must have had some party. She steeled herself against the picture of two perfect bodies coming together in a passionate embrace.

Digger would eat up this kind of gossip . . . except she wasn't going to tell him privileged material. She was no snoop. Digger would get only what Steven told her in an interview. The most she was prepared to say was that Steven obviously liked women. Too much!

The love goddess spoke; Holly cringed. "When I get home later, snookums, I promise to straighten up."

Holly was so taken aback by Louise's term for

Steven she completely missed the grim look he shot at her. All she heard was his response.

"You'd better. I lost my maid. Liz," he said, drawing her into the conversation for the first time, "do you happen to know of anyone who wants a job?"

Snookums! She could think of a lot of things to call Steven—snookums wasn't one of them. Her lips twitched. She giggled. His eyes blazed. She shrugged her shoulders. He squeezed her fingers.

"Forgive me," she sputtered merrily. "I was thinking about something, snookums." The darkening color in his cheeks told Holly she had hit home.

Louise kissed his cheek. "Steven isn't the world's neatest person, are you, precious?"

Snookums? Precious? Holly's shoulders shook with mirth. She tried to pull her hand out of Steven's, who was taking great pleasure, she knew, in seeing how hard he could squeeze without breaking her fingers. Suppressing a laugh, she lifted her lashes and stared wide-eyed into his angry features.

"If I happen to meet anyone who's looking for a job, I'll be only too glad to pass your name along. I imagine the fringe benefits must be terrific."

He glared at her murderously. "What do you mean by that?"

Louise interrupted. "Oh, don't fuss so, Steven. You're a positive grouch in the mornings. I'm going to help you find a maid. I don't suppose you thought to post a notice on the bulletin board? Many of the help here check on it for friends. In fact, if you're very nice to me, I might even consent to conduct the interview for you."

Hugging her shoulder, he smiled brightly. "I'll be eternally grateful. So will my doctor. You know what he said about stress."

"*Mmmm.* How eternal? How grateful? You remember the private matter we spoke about? If I do this for you, I expect a favor in return, something to relieve *my* stress. You get my drift, don't you?"

We all do, Holly thought, feigning nonchalance. She couldn't wait to get out of there. Then Snookums and Louise could make kissy-poo all they wanted. At least she wouldn't be around to watch!

She reported her meager findings to Digger over lunch at Trader Vic's, keeping to her personal ethical code and not revealing any of the really juicy personal information. Now he'd release her, she was sure. Constantly at work, Digger gushed over a current female star, waved to another, and finally gave Holly his attention.

"Let's see what we can salvage from this," he said, dashing her hopes for a quick solution that would keep her job intact, but relieve her of what Digger euphemistically termed *investigative reporting.* "When you told me what happened on the elevator, I thought for sure you'd blown it. But the business about his needing a maid has possibilities."

"You're going to hire a maid to spy on him?"

Digger shook his head, brushing aside her statement. He put his fork on his plate and announced his latest brainstorm. "I'm not hiring anyone. *You're* going to be the maid. It's perfect."

Holly's eyes opened wide. She willed herself to contain her panic, to reason with Digger. "That's impossible. Haven't you heard a word I've said? He knows me as Liz Mason, complete with a damned wig! Besides, you knew my feelings about this whole operation in the first place," she pleaded. He even had her thinking in spy lingo!

Digger reached over and grabbed her hand. His eyes held the fire of inspiration. "I heard everything you said. I *do* understand," he said soothingly. "I'll hire an actress to go on the job interview instead of you. Believe me, in this town, they'd do anything to get their name in my column."

"Except Steven Chadwick," she reminded him. If her remark registered, Digger gave no notice. He was eager to get on with his plan.

"Chadwick won't see you. You don't expect him to stay home every time a maid comes to clean, do you? He'll probably leave a key, the way we all do for our help."

Her food was starting to form a knot in her stomach. She knew where Digger's mind was racing. All she could do now was stay and listen to the rest of his wild plan. Tonight, she'd start searching through the want ads for another job.

"Wouldn't it be simpler to put another researcher on the case?"

He shook his head. "Too much money. Besides,

I can't spare anyone else. Let me remind you, Chadwick's your bachelor."

Mine and Louise's. She was getting numb. "What's the plan?" she asked.

Flashing a smile of considerable warmth, Digger held court. "You mentioned that the woman he introduced you to—a Louise—has offered to conduct the interview for him?"

"Yes."

"What's the relationship there?" he asked suddenly.

"He told me they've known each other from childhood, and that he loves her."

"Platonically?"

"Yes. He said he loves her like a sister." She knew better! She was sure they were sleeping together. Steven was probably protecting her privacy as much as he was protecting his own. They might, in fact, be planning on marriage. Providing, of course, they could find a maid! She couldn't see Snookum's ladylove pushing a vacuum!

"Then he's still fair game, but be sure of that before I write his segment of the book. Oh, never mind," he said, changing his on the spot, "just get all the information about Chadwick you can. I'll decide what to do with it."

"Can't we discuss this?" she argued, feeling more and more distressed. "The man has a right to his privacy. Surely if you're patient and let me approach him, I'll be able to come up with something for you without going though all this subterfuge."

Digger very deliberately picked up his knife, symbolically cutting her off. "My dear Holly, if patience were the name of the game, there'd be no need for deadlines. Do I make myself clear?"

Too clear! she thought, frantically searching for a way to block Digger off at the pass. Pass. She was even beginning to think like Steven! Next thing she knew she'd be wearing cowboy boots and packing a gun in a holster!

Digger signaled for the check; Holly was all too glad to get the luncheon over with. They strolled outside into the brilliant sunshine. It was the kind of smog-free day travel agents dream of. Warm, with a trace of the sea in the air.

Before parting, Digger paused on the sidewalk to finish his instructions. "Since you're going to do the actual work, I think it would be best if the cover story the actress feeds Louise—or Chadwick, if he decides to conduct the interview—allows you to clean at your convenience. Don't you agree?"

In a flash of revelation, Holly saw a way to thwart Digger's plan. She really would head him off at the pass. *She* would become Steven's protector! "Definitely," she agreed, thrilled to finally figure out a way to guard Steven's interests. Besides, if she disagreed, Digger would fill her place with someone else—the actress, probably. Someone more than willing to do Digger's bidding in return for a favorable mention in his column. It was the least she could do to return Steven's kindness.

"Good. By the way, Holly, there's an A party I might ask you to cover for me."

"An A party?" *They alphabetized parties?*

Digger shook his head at her provincialism. "Minneapolis! I don't know why I waste my time with you! An A-list party, as opposed to a B or C list, is the party everyone in town simply dies to get an invitation to. Naturally, I'm invited to all of them," he bragged.

She smiled carefully. Digger set great store by lists. "Then I hope you have a good time." She couldn't imagine anything more frivolous than worrying about which list you were on.

He sensed her reproach. "I don't think you understand my meaning at all. Marte Cudworth is throwing a bash at her estate for Louise Armand's latest film—"

"Louise Armand is an actress? That's the Louise I was talking about!"

He stared at her, incredulous. "What world do you live in?"

"I usually see foreign films," she meekly apologized. No wonder Louise's face was familiar. Now she was more convinced of her theory than ever. Steven couldn't love Louise as a sister; she was too beautiful, too glamorous, too everything Holly was not. His explanation was all a bunch of baloney! He just wanted to protect their relationship until he and Louise were ready to announce their nuptials to the public. It certainly would be right in character.

"When you mentioned Louise's name, I remembered the invitation. Steven Chadwick is on the list. If he goes, I'll send you. You'll blend into the background beautifully. Think of the opportunity to get firsthand gossip."

"How did you know his name was on the list?"

Digger could barely contain his annoyance. "My dear girl, give me credit for something!"

She marveled at Digger's network of spies. It included secretaries, doctors, lawyers, housekeepers, shopkeepers, food vendors, even sanitary engineers.

She could see the letter she planned to write home tonight.

Dear Mom and Dad,

The job is great. All the money you spent on my college education was worth it. I begin my duties as a cleaning woman any day now. At least I get to wear my own hair!

Love,
Holly

Four

Steven's definition of friendship was driving Holly up the wall. He was fun. He was charming. He was there.

As a friend to Liz.

As a protector to Liz.

As a lecturer to Liz.

"You missed your calling," she grumbled when he announced it was time for her exercise program to begin. "You'd make an excellent drill sergeant."

He took it as a compliment. She threw up her hands and followed him out the door for a walk.

Trotting alongside, trying to adjust to his loping strides, she thought about her unique circumstances. She had scrupulously avoided asking him any questions, even the innocent ones friends would ask, because she didn't want to mix friendship and business. She hadn't even asked him about the scar near his mouth, although she was dying to know how he'd gotten it.

And something was happening to her. He was like a powerful drug—the more she saw him, the more she wanted to be with him. To listen to his laugh—a deep rumble that rose in his chest and burst forth with joy. To argue with him about proper nutrition. It turned out his knowledge was indeed lousy—no wonder the doctor had warned him about an ulcer. To wait for him while he exercised. To imagine him coming home to her each night. To fantasize being in his arms, loving him, kissing him . . .

From time to time she would catch his blue gaze fixed on her, and she would feel absurdly happy. His mouth fascinated her. His lips were strong, yet sensual—the kind a woman conjured up in her dreams.

And there wasn't a thing she could do about it!

He wasn't hers.

Because of finances, she had gotten herself embroiled in an impossible situation. It was like walking through a maze with no exit. Even if she returned to Minneapolis, she had no job. She wouldn't think of sponging off of her parents, or her brother Mark. She couldn't go home a failure.

Each day she poured through the newspapers to see if anyone wanted someone with her qualifications. She had already left her resumé at various employment agencies and universities. The answer was always the same: no openings now, but something might turn up. Don't call us, we'll call you.

She was juggling her life like a tightrope walker. With each checking phone call, Digger sounded more and more suspicious of her personal motives. "Is there something going on between you two?" he'd ask accusingly. Having heard Digger brag about the methods he employed to get his information, she kept up with the charade. She couldn't leave Steven in the lurch.

"Steven, I've got to talk to you," she said one night when it had gotten too much for her.

"Hush, hon. Can it wait? We're coming to the best part." They were watching one of Lance Trainor's movies. Or, rather, Steven was. His eyes were glued to the television screen. Hers were glued to him. The urge to touch him was irresistible. He had come to her door unexpectedly, looking for all the world as if he were Santa Claus's helper. He was ecstatic, beaming. He'd carried a bowl of caramel popcorn in one hand and two Lance Trainor movies in the other. He dropped a kiss on her cheek, breezed past her into the room, and began speaking excitedly.

"These weren't easy to locate. Do you know how many stores don't carry his films?"

She could just imagine!

He was so proud of himself—so ridiculously happy—she didn't have the heart to ruin his evening. He had brought the films over to share with her. How could she burst his bubble? Their serious talk would have to wait.

The next time she tried to explain her situation,

everything that *could* go wrong went wrong—starting with her burning her mouth on hot, spicy food, and Steven needing her help to relieve the pain of a toothache! It was as if someone were gleefully saying *Gotcha!*, thwarting her at every turn.

Steven had phoned unexpectedly, telling her not to eat dinner—he was bringing in. He knocked on her door with a full-course Mexican meal and a bouquet of huge yellow, red, orange, and green paper flowers for atmosphere. He had even produced a couple of Mexican jumping beans for authenticity, tickled pink when they jumped over themselves. Holly rolled her eyes heavenward. She never knew when he was going to pull these crazy stunts. Steven, she had learned, loved surprises.

It also occurred to her that he always expected her to be home.

Dateless.

He was dressed in a pair of old blue jeans that did nothing to hide the strength of his thigh muscles. His blue shirt matched his eyes. He could, she decided, be dressed like bum: he'd still be a knockout.

"Steven . . ."—she felt like a dragon breathing fire from the spicy food—". . . after dinner, we've got to talk."

"Fine," he said cheerfully. He reached for more hot salsa.

Desire and discretion warred within her; desire fought to shout out the truth and be done with it, discretion warned her to go easy. If she yielded to her natural instinct, Steven would react like a charging bull.

She gulped another glass of water. "This has to rank as the hottest Mexican food ever."

"Terrific, isn't it? I'm glad you like it. Have some more."

"I thought you said you were cooking an ulcer," she gasped.

"False alarm. Must have been stress." Then he screamed.

"What's the matter?" Holly jumped out of her seat, rushing over to him. Squirming in his chair, he pointed to the side of his jaw.

"Dentist," he yelped painfully. "I . . . I . . . just came from the dentist."

Holly shook her head. She knew exactly what had happened. "And," she finished, "the dentist told you not to eat on that side. Right?"

Steven bobbed his head up and down. "I swear," she muttered, heading for the refrigerator. "You're a kid. You'd think a grown man would have more sense." She wrapped some ice in a washcloth. "Give me your hand."

"My hand?" he said thickly, offering his hand to her.

She began to massage the curve of his palm between his thumb and his pointer finger. She kept this up for about five minutes, until Steven stopped moaning. "Acu-ice," she explained, seeing his flabbergasted expression. "It's a form of acupuncture. That spot controls the side of your jaw."

Amazed that she was able to take the pain away,

he said, "You're terrific. You know, you're good for me, Liz."

She could feel her heart slam against her ribs. Holly's and Liz's identities were blurring in her mind. At night she lay in bed dreaming erotic dreams of being more than a friend to Steven. It wasn't meant to be, she knew. Steven spent so much time with her because Louise was a busy actress. Aside from a hug or a kiss, he kept their friendship platonic. The perfect gentleman!

She often wondered why he never invited her up to his apartment; then she realized Louise must have laid down the law and said, "I draw the line at bringing your little mouse up here!"

"Why am I good for you?" she asked finally. She half-expected him to teasingly drop one of his ribald remarks.

He gazed at her, trying to define his feelings. She *was* good for him, he realized with a shock. The words that had slipped out had not been said in jest.

He could laugh with her. He could talk to her. He could bring his pain to her. Most of all, he could be quiet with her. He knew her fears—and respected them. He enjoyed his bachelorhood, and she made no demands on him. He'd never felt so at ease or so protective of a woman in his life. If once or twice he felt a pang of guilt because he was taking up too much of her time, he dismissed it by telling himself she seemed content too. There she sat, with those wonderful hazel eyes, saucily waiting for his answer.

What could he tell her? She wasn't anything

like the glamorous women he dated. Should he tell her that although she didn't dress in the latest style, it didn't matter? When he was with her, it didn't matter what she wore. The women he dated spent an allowance on clothes that Liz didn't earn in a year. Looking beneath the surface to the soul of a person is what counts. She was far more than surface. Liz was Liz. Earnest, sweet, fun to be with—and feisty.

"Did you forget the question?" she asked softly. Before she realized it, she had reached her hand across the table. One last time to pretend.

He smiled and turned her palm over. Impulsively, he dropped a kiss at the base of her thumb, sending little darts of pleasure through her.

"You're easy to be with, Liz. You're a decent, hardworking, honest woman. You're a terrific doctor. I can be myself with you. You'd be surprised how many women aren't what they pretend to be."

Drowning in the depths of his serious blue eyes, Holly wanted to slide under the table. He was assigning his steadfast, honorable qualities to her. As unobtrusively as possible, she withdrew her hand. Even after she did, it still felt branded.

"Steven, there's something I have to tell you about me."

"Don't tell me you're going to confess you're not who you claim to be?"

She gasped. "How did you know?"

"It's simple, really. You've been trying to come off as an independent career woman ever since I met you. The truth is, you're wondering about giving up your career."

"No, as a matter of fact, I love my career—most of the time. I haven't been exactly aboveboard with—"

Her confession was interrupted by a phone call; Digger must have sensed she was ready to throw in the towel. When she hung up, Steven was yawning. Apologizing, he told her he had an early appointment.

"Please, this won't take long."

He threw his jacket down on the couch. "Do you mind?" he asked, slipping off his loafers. He eased himself down on the sofa. He propped a pillow behind his head, then held out his hand to her. "Thanks, Liz."

"For what?" she asked huskily.

"For nothing. Just for being you. For making the toothache go away. Go ahead," he said pleasantly. "Let's hear what's on your mind."

She choked up. What woman wouldn't cherish a man like him? He was so good . . . so kind . . . and so grateful when she soothed away his pain. She only hoped he'd be forgiving too.

Looking at him, she knew she needed fortification. Her throat was drying up. "I'll be back in a minute." She dashed into the kitchen for a glass of water. When she came back into the room, he beckoned her to sit near him.

"Go ahead, I'm listening."

She sat on the edge of the chair opposite him and began speaking, paving the way for recent developments by touching on parts of her previous life. She explained why she had left Minneapolis. He told her he understood her quest for more excitement, more fulfillment in her job. He particularly wanted to know about the boy who had locked her into the refrigerator, telling her he wanted to punch the guy's lights out.

"I'm sure he doesn't remember it now. It's been a long time."

"Maybe, but I hate him anyway. Look what he's done to you. I'm glad I was in that elevator with you, Liz."

Holly's heart tripped. She loved Steven for his concern, so much so that she found she couldn't face those blue eyes burning into hers. She wasn't quite brave enough to have him watch her when she came to the part that would end their friendship. Getting up, she walked toward the window.

"I promise not to ask any more questions until you're through," he said.

She smiled, then explained how excited she had been when she had landed the job working for Digger, thinking it would magically transport her into a whole new world. She poured out her story, telling him everything. When she came to the part about the maid, her voice faltered. "Believe me, Steven, I only wanted to protect you. You don't know how a man like Digger operates. . . ."

From the other side of the room she turned, wanting to see his reaction. His hand was flung over his forehead, covering his eyes. *He's so disappointed in me he can't even look at me!* she thought bitterly. Gentleman to the last, he had refrained from interrupting.

Sighing deeply, she continued, her voice strong at times, faltering at others. She continued to pace in front of the window, wringing her small hands for emphasis.

"So you see,"—she pleaded for understanding—"I couldn't let a stranger enter your apartment and rifle through your belongings. You've been so good to me. Please, Steven, regardless of what you must be feeling for me, let me give Digger something. If you don't, he'll hire someone else—that's why I've been trying to interview you. You'll never know who the person is, either." She began to feel frantic. "It might even be your garage mechanic.

"Can you ever forgive me?" she asked softly, coming close for his reaction. She waited, sick with anticipation, breathless for the verdict.

A soft snore answered her question.

Her eyes darted over him; his chest was rising and falling in deep contentment. She picked up the arm draped over his forehead. When she let it go, it flopped back down like a rag doll's. His eyelids were shut tight. There was a smile on his face. She wanted to tear his hair out.

"You can't be asleep, dammit! I just poured out my guts to you and you slept through my confession!" she wailed.

"Steven," she said sharply, "wake up!"

He snored again.

Drained beyond belief, she was on the verge of tears. She bent down, grabbed him by the shoulders, and shook him. For her efforts, she heard the man to whom she had just delivered the speech of a lifetime mumble something about blondes.

What kind of a secret life did he live? Dreaming about blondes! Louise was a redhead! She was a—

temporary—brunette! Who, she thought with murder in her eye, is the blonde?

"Steven, wake up. It's time to go home."

"Ooops," he said sheepishly. "Sorry. I guess I conked out. This couch is comfortable. I could have slept here all night." He rolled to a sitting position, stood up, and stretched.

"What am I going to do with you?" Holly wailed.

"Come here." He drew her into his arms and hugged her close to his chest. "Forgive me, Liz." He kissed her temple. "What did you want to talk about?" He yawned again.

She was ready to scream. "Did you hear one word I said?"

"Sure," he said, looking like an adorable, rumpled mess. "You told me all about the bastard who locked you in the refrigerator, and how you wanted to come to California for excitement. I still want to break the guy's nose for scaring you."

She groaned. The gods were conspiring against her. "You missed the best part, you big dope."

"Do you want me to stay?" he asked, trying unsuccessfully to stifle a big yawn.

"No. It'll keep." She couldn't put herself through that speech twice in one evening. Besides, Steven was out on his feet. But next time she'd hold his eyelids open with toothpicks if she had to. Or maybe she should stand him under a cold shower. On second thought, if she ever saw him in a shower, she wouldn't be able to talk.

At the door, he turned to hug her again. The pain of being in his arms was bittersweet. It was all she could do not to reach up and draw his lips down to hers.

Later, Holly recalled the sound of his heartbeat, the strength of his arms, the brush of his cheek on hers, the whisper of his breath in her ear asking her to forgive him for falling asleep.

"Oh, Steven," she whispered into the night, "you'll never know how difficult this is for me." Maybe, she thought, exhausted from her ordeal, she should just write him a letter—and mail it from the North Pole!

Her intentions were good. The next day, at his insistence, she accompanied him to the park while he jogged. The sun was shining, it was early in the morning, and he was wide awake. She had the whole thing planned. She even skipped break-fast because—if last night was any indication of how her stomach reacted during Truth or Cons-equences—she was better off not eating. She also decided to let him go for his run first. That way he'd be pooped, or at least winded, while she hur-ried through her speech. Then he'd be off to work.

Timing was everything!

It didn't work.

Steven wasn't his usual self. He was very preoc-cupied, very worried about business. He had re-ceived a phone call that upset him greatly. Taking her into his confidence, he unburdened his heart of his problems. He was trying to figure out a way to transfer some of his workers to different sites so they wouldn't lose their jobs. He explained how complicated this would be, but that he had in-structed his people to try.

"At least some of the men will bring in a paycheck."

Although he had nothing to do with the building moratorium, he felt responsible, since he had hired these people. He told her he would be leaving in an hour for Santos. When he told her he would be spending the weekend at his home in Oxnard, she felt a pang of loss, but held back from letting him see her reaction. He was beat mentally, and needed a change of scenery. A day at sea, away from the telephones would do him good. With a heavy heart, she realized it was not an opportune time to add to his problems. What he needed now was a friend he could trust. At least for a little while longer she could be that friend, and protect his interests from Digger's clever machinations.

"Hi, been waiting long?" Stephen asked when he returned from his jog.

Holly's heart jumped. She drew in her breath; he was so handsome. There was more than one reason she didn't want Digger to write about him in his book. Any woman in her right mind would love to have a man like Steven. With his blue eyes shining and his hair backlit by the sun, he looked to Holly like a young Hercules. She put on her brightest smile. Holding up the magazine she had been reading, she nodded. "Time flies when you're having fun."

He bent over, grabbing his ankles. "Next week, you ought to start jogging with me."

Holly wasn't listening. She was too busy noticing another one of his good features—his nice, tight tush. He stood up, repeated himself, then caught her looking. He grinned.

"Did you hear me, woman? I said it's time to move your butt." He removed the sweatband from his forehead and began his cool-down exercises.

"But, Steven," she said, watching the muscles ripple in his arms, "I get exhausted just watching you jog. That's enough exercise for me!"

Laughing, he swatted her arm with his towel. "Sassy mouth." He continued to cool down by stretching out his leg and thigh muscles against the wooden bench. When he was through, he lay down on the grass, looking up at her. Awareness of him flowed through her in a rush of desire.

He rolled over onto his stomach. His hand idly stroked her leg, exploding little fires along the path his fingers took. "Steven," she pleaded. "Go to Santos." *Then come back,* she said silently, *and I'll straighten out this mess.*

He bounced up and wiped the grass off his legs. Tilting her chin up, he gazed into her troubled little face and was ashamed of himself. He had been selfish, imposing himself on her, using her for a sounding board, taking her friendship and not giving enough in return. She had been helping him without knowing it. Now, if she had a problem, the least he could do would be to return the favor.

"Liz, friends help friends. I promise to be here for you. I just wish I didn't have to leave so soon, or we'd continue our talk now. Don't worry—we'll work it out together."

She looked at his dear face, then closed her eyes

and prayed it would bé so. Why couldn't he have come out with one of his clever remarks? *That* she could deal with. She sighed. Just once, she yearned to put her head on his chest and snuggle the way she had in the elevator. She ran her finger along his jawline. "Thank you for offering. The problem will resolve itself soon anyway."

Two hours later, Digger informed Holly that the actress pretending to be the maid had been interviewed and hired by Louise. The maid was due to begin her duties tomorrow, when Holly knew Steven would be away. With a sinking feeling, Holly knew if she didn't take the job as the maid, the actress Digger hired would. Determined not to allow Steven's private life to be dragged into print without his permission, she had only one choice.

To protect the man she loved, Holly/Liz would also become Hortense the maid! *Will I ever find a way out of this mess?*

Five

The Chadwick Building in Century City housed
the West Coast headquarters of the multimillion-
dollar architectural design and construction firm,
Chadwick, Inc. On the wall near Steven's desk
hung his diploma from the Yale School of Architecture.

Steven pulled a blueprint from the rack. He
walked over to the drafting table in his office to
check on a design for a high rise to be constructed
in Chicago. His business had always been his
primary interest since he'd begun it on a shoe-
string following graduation. He had respectfully
refused the venture capital his father offered, pre-
ferring to do it himself. All of it. He doggedly
insisted on experiencing the pitfalls and the joys
of climbing up the ladder on his own. And climb
he did. His innovative, money-saving designs had
found an acceptance beyond his wildest hopes.

Solving the problem in Santos he had discussed with Liz earlier meant a great deal to him. Chadwick's was busier than ever, and while he could personally weather the financial storms the Santos situation would create, the workers could not. He was as much concerned for them as anything else. Liz had understood that too.

He stared thoughtfully into space, thinking about her. How it had happened he didn't know, but she had gotten under his skin.

Returning to work, he forced himself to keep his mind on business. Finishing with one set of drawings, he went to the rack for another. Spreading it out on the table, he checked the blueprints of the hotel complex and convention center his company would be building in Baltimore.

Satisfied with the drawings, he went over to his computer and sat down. There, he recalled drawings he had previously digitized. He examined one of the buildings to check its rotation design. Working steadily, he quickly modified a grid in its reflective ceiling. In seconds, twenty identical grids repeated themselves in one direction, and fifty in another.

Now why, he mused, couldn't his other problems be solved as quickly? He turned off the computer and returned to his desk, where he drew out a portfolio containing the file on his Santos project.

There had been a last-minute change in plans; instead of being gone overnight, he had to be away for a week. He was now scheduled to go to New York City and Baltimore before returning to

California. Larry would meet him later on in the week in Santos.

"Cheer up," Larry had told him. Besides being his corporate attorney, he was also his friend. "I think there's a small ray of hope."

Thinking of Larry made him think of Louise and her offer to help interview a maid. He could probably have phoned an agency himself, but he felt more confident with Louise conducting the interview. Knowing she wasn't due on the set today, he picked up the phone and dialed her number.

"Any luck?" he asked.

It was eleven in the morning. Her voice sounded clogged with sleep. "With what? My helping you find a maid, or you helping Larry find wedded bliss?"

"One of these days, he's bound to come around," he said with more encouragement than he felt.

"Do you think so?" Louise's voice was surprisingly shy.

"Bet money on it. Now, what do you have to report to me? Any luck with the agency or the bulletin board?"

She sounded more awake now. "Yes, on both counts. I interviewed the nicest lady. Her name is Hortense Shaw. Maybe you should interview her too. After all, it's your home."

"Louise, I trust you. Tell me about her."

"She's about fifty—salt-and-pepper gray hair. She looks strong. I had to agree to certain terms. If you don't approve, I'll give you her number. You can change it yourself."

"What terms?" he asked, alert now.

"Hortense attends college. Her children are grown. She's divorced. She promises to come in two times a week to start with. If you need her more, work it out yourself with her. About the hours: if you'll give her a key—"

"Is she bonded—insured? In case something goes wrong? Most companies send out bonded help; it's a protection for both parties."

"I never asked. Really, Steven, the woman who works for me isn't bonded either."

"All right. I guess I can't look a gift horse in the mouth. When can Hortense start?"

"She made a particular point about that, because she'll only come in when her study schedule is light. She said you can leave each other notes if there's anything special you need or if she's out of supplies."

He perched on the edge of his desk, then flipped on the intercom to finish the rest of the conversation while he went to the window to watch the world go by. He felt restless.

"Sounds like she's very ambitious. You have to give her credit for returning to school. Did she furnish references?"

"Naturally," Louise said. "I checked them out myself. Apparently, you've hit a winner. Better stay on her good side."

"*Mmmm.*" His attention was caught by a dainty, brunette woman who resembled Liz. Or maybe he just had Liz on his mind and was seeing her in every dark-haired woman? She was dressed in a navy blue suit and low-heeled shoes. Interested, he followed her with his eyes.

"Where did you tell Hortense I'd leave the key?" he asked, watching out the window as the woman crossed the street.

"In the usual place. Was that all right?"

The petite brunette paused on the sidewalk. He saw a dapperly dressed man emerge from a taxi-cab. Curious, Steven watched the byplay. The brunette handed the man an envelope, then the man kissed her on the lips, took her elbow, and helped her into the cab.

The entire incident couldn't have lasted more than a minute, yet the hairs on the back of his neck prickled. He didn't like the vibes he was getting. A sharp whistle brought his attention back to the phone call.

"I asked, are you satisfied?"

"Sure," he said. His eyes continued to track the cab until it disappeared in traffic. *Could that have been Liz?* he wondered. "Ahh . . . thanks, Louise. I appreciate it."

"You know how to show your appreciation," Louise countered.

"Okay. You win," he said, giving his attention back to Louise. "And I'm not doing it because of Hortense. I'm doing it because I think you and Larry are good for each other."

She laughed. "Good-bye, Steve. I wish you a long and happy life with Hortense."

"Considering we'll probably be two ships that pass in the night, your wish will come true."

Was the woman Liz? he kept wondering. If she was, it was none of his business. If Liz chose to go out with Methuselah, it would still be none of his business.

Louise had called him a cynic; maybe he was. Still, it seemed a shame for Liz—assuming it *was* Liz—to waste her youth on a man old enough to be her father.

He dismissed the whole idea from his mind and went to an executive staff meeting. The moment the meeting ended, he told his secretary he'd be back shortly, and left. He rode the elevator down to the subterranean garage and unlocked the door to his car. He gunned the Ferrari. Fifteen minutes later he was striding through the lobby of his building.

Once inside the elevator, he punched the number twelve, quite prepared to punch someone's face if the damned thing didn't work. By the time his finger was on the bell outside Liz's apartment, he had worked up a good head of steam. The only measure of comfort he found was in hearing music through the door. She was home.

"Who is it?"

"Steve," he yelled.

Holly's hands flew to her head. *Steven couldn't be out there. He's supposed to be in Santos!* What was he doing here? Frantically, her eyes darted to the coffee table covered with pictures, old magazines, newspaper clippings, and other background information about the Chadwick family. She had decided to be prepared in case Steven would agree to an interview. During the past two days, except for her luncheon engagement with Digger, she had been holed up in her own apartment in North Hollywood, working. She had even begun to write some preliminary copy—reworking information already published about the Chadwick's—for Digger. Today, Digger had mistakenly assumed that the envelope she had handed him contained important information about Steven. Much to her disgust, Digger had even kissed her.

"Are you going to open the door or what?" Steven called.

"Just a minute. I'm indisposed. Give me a sec."

While he remained outside, Holly flew around the room, shoving the once neatly organized papers into a trash bag. She dashed into the bedroom and banged her knee on the edge of the bed frame as she shoved the bag beneath the bed.

She stood up and started running, then slid back on her heels in a dead stop as she caught a glimpse of herself in the mirror.

"My hair!" she gasped. It was the wrong color! She yanked the wig off the dressing table and, working feverishly, tugged it down over her head. Her fingers worked frantically to hide the strands of blond hair.

Holly opened the door to a pair of sapphirelike eyes sweeping over her accusingly.

"What the hell took you so long?" He wasn't hallucinating—she *was* the brunette he had seen kissing the old geek.

"I wasn't dressed. What are you doing home?" she asked cautiously. "I thought you were out of town." Something must have happened since this morning; he looked positively livid. She smiled a nervous little smile. *He can't come home in the afternoons. He's supposed to be a creature of habit. It's going to louse up everything!*

She eyed him uncertainly. "I . . . I . . . mean—what are you doing *here*?"

He pushed past her into the living room. He didn't see any evidence of other visitors, but he still didn't trust her. The little fool needed him more than ever.

"I work fifteen minutes from here. Aren't I allowed to come home if I want to? Anyway, my plans changed. I came home for a briefcase I need to take with me on my trip. I thought I'd say good-bye."

She grabbed hold of his arm and propelled him back in the direction of the door. "Good-bye, then. As you can see, I'm working."

"No," he said, shrugging her hand off his arm, "I *can't* see, as a matter of fact. Why are you so jumpy?" *He knew damn well why! He never would have believed it of her—making out with a man old enough to be her father, for goodness' sake!*

"Just a minute." He forced himself to sound amiable. "I have a little while before I have to go. How about fixing me a drink?" He strolled past her and sat down on the couch; he spread his arms wide on the top of the couch and strummed his fingers.

Stop acting guilty, Holly told herself. *You haven't done anything.* "What would you like to drink?"

"Whatever you're having."

What in the world was wrong with him? "But I'm not drinking."

"Oh, come now," he said. A ghost of a smile touched his face. "Surely we can find something to celebrate. We can celebrate our friendship." She stared at him. "No," he said, changing his mind. "I'll tell you what. Let's celebrate my hiring a new maid. Or, rather, Louise's hiring me a new maid."

Terrific! Now she was supposed to drink to herself! She couldn't fathom his mood. To all outward appearances, he was the same. But she knew better—he was furious about something.

"How's Louise?" she asked, handing him a scotch and water.

He took the glass from her, tilting it up in a salute before taking a sip. He peered at her over the rim. "Fine, as far as I know. If you need more information, you'll have to ask Larry."

"Who's Larry?"

"The man she wants to marry. He's also my best friend and corporate lawyer."

Holly didn't hear anything beyond the fact that Louise was in love with someone else. Her heart sang with joy. Then, just as quickly, she wondered whether Steven had thrown that out as a smoke screen. It wouldn't be the first time a prominent person had floated a cover story.

"What'd you do today, Liz?" he asked in a friendly tone.

Holly's joy was tempered by Steven's strange behavior. She was peculiarly conscious of his unwavering gaze. "I worked," she answered honestly.

He inclined his head. Then he rose, pacing the room like a caged animal.

"Sit down, for goodness' sake, before you spill the drink on the carpet."

"Where are you working?" he asked pleasantly. He looked around the neat room. "You're home early too, aren't you?"

Why the inquisition? She needed time to think. She went to the bar to pour herself a soft drink, her mind clicking like a metronome. Tell him—don't tell him. She peeled off the reasons to tell him everything. Then she canceled them out, knowing Steven was about to leave for a trip. Her mouth felt dry.

"I came home to think out a problem."

"The same problem you were worried about in the park?" he asked as he moved toward her. The smoothness of his voice was completely at odds with the ice-blue of his eyes.

"Yes," she said truthfully. Better to get her confession over and done with. The hell with worrying about how he'd take it. He was a big boy, and dammit, she hadn't done anything except try to protect his pigheaded self! She was tired of sitting on a time bomb.

"Yes," she said. She dismissed a slight prickle of uneasiness when Steven moved closer to her. She would lead into Digger's plan and her part in it carefully, because Steven looked angry enough to explode before she had a chance to say a word.

"Actually, it's about my boss—the man I tried to tell you about last night, but you slept through it. We met for lunch today. There's a problem."

Steven's muscles tensed. He knew it! The little nut was throwing herself away on the old jerk! Did she think she wasn't good enough to get a man closer to her age? What did she see in him?

"What's his name?"

"His name is Daniel Danville," she blurted out. "There's something he wants me to do. Actually, it's more than *one* something." Oh, dear; it was so much easier talking to a sleeping bear than a wide-awake one.

Steven closed his eyes. He was filled with rage. From what he had seen today, she was quite happy to do whatever that old man wanted her to. Well, he wasn't going to let her play him for a sucker. He had been a fool to think she was any different from most women who schemed to get what they wanted.

"Liz—stop lying. You don't have to pretend."

Holly's head jerked up. At first she wasn't sure she had heard him correctly. The moment their gazes locked, she knew she had. Her hand flew to her breast; her eyes—wide and apprehensive—filled with tears. The jig was up! The confession was unnecessary. Steven knew, and was furious. Somehow . . . someway . . . he had found out about the wild scheme Digger had cooked up. It must have been Louise. She was a movie star. Of course! She'd know Digger! Why, her name had no doubt been in his column many times.

Steven hated her. It was plain to see by the anger in his eyes. Well, he couldn't put her in jail for wearing a wig and telling him her last name was Mason. She'd never once set foot in his apartment. All she could be accused of was trying to help him!

"I know all about it," he said coldly.

He knows and he's stringing me along. In-

stead of coming straight out with it like a gentle-man, he's actually enjoying my misery. Holly's quick temper took hold. She wasn't about to grovel for forgiveness; he'd have to go somewhere else for his pound of flesh. She had been through enough hell trying to tap-dance around Digger and not lose her job. She wasn't going to hang her head like a drowned rat. No, sir. If she had to take her medicine, she would do so with her chin up.

"How—how did you find out?" Her hand had started to move up to yank off the wig when Steven's next words stopped her dead.

"I saw you with him today. I saw you with your lover."

"My *what*!" she screeched.

"Yes. I saw that old man kiss you, and I saw you kiss him back. I saw you get into a cab with him. He's not your boss, is he? He's your lover."

She shook her head in wonder. Here was a new side to Steven—he was acting like a jealous bull at mating time. The nut saw her with Digger, drew his brilliant conclusion, and assumed Digger was her lover!

How could they have been so careless? Easy. She had thought Steven was out of town. She hadn't thought to be cautious when she met Digger, and Digger's innocent kiss was just his exuberant way of telling her how pleased he was that the maid had been hired.

"He's *not* my lover," she said truthfully, trying to diffuse some of the steam sizzling around them.

So—she was ashamed to tell him. Ashamed for

him to lend credence to what his own eyes had seen. He hunted for the right words. "Liz," Steven explained quietly, "you're not an ugly woman. You don't have to settle for an old man. All you have to do is change your hairstyle, maybe dress a little more stylishly. I'm sure you'll find a man nearer your age." *It might even be me*—but now wasn't the time to plead his case. She was too overwrought.

"*What?*" Holly screamed so loudly the teacups on the table rattled. She couldn't believe his gall! Here she was, ready to do penance—and for what? For not doing what she had been hired to do, so as not to have a guilty conscience, in a town where it was commonplace to do it anyway! And furthermore! She had beat the pavement, leaving her resumé all over town. She had even considered going back home, where her parents would love her *regardless!* And what did she get in return for her high moral standards? For her nobility? A kick in the pants, that's what! She was so mad she saw every color of the rainbow.

She hauled off and slapped his face.

"You conceited beast. Thanks for telling me I don't know how to dress. Thanks for telling me I don't know how to style my hair." Privately, she agreed with him—she had known the damned wig would be her undoing. She slapped his hand away when he tried to capture hers.

"Dammit." He grabbed her shoulders and shook her. "I meant it for your welfare. Why are you throwing yourself at a man old enough to be your father?"

Fine. He wanted to hear about her boyfriend—

she'd tell him. "He's fifty-eight. Hardly in the grave. He's fun and—"

"Then why aren't you seeing him in the evenings? You've never mentioned him. I've been here—" His face held a look of dawning shock. "My God, you're having an affair with a married man, aren't you? That's what you've been trying to tell me."

Holly was as near hysterics as she'd ever been in her life. She was still bristling over the fact that he thought her one step up from ugly. "No, it isn't! And I'll have you know that what I do in my private life is *my* business, Steven Chadwick, not yours."

She pushed past him, bumping into a chair in her path. She cursed. "I can't get over it." She was talking rapidly, incensed. "Here I worried because I wasn't being honest, didn't tell you about myself—"

"But you did. It isn't your fault I fell asleep last night. Just because I saw you with the old geek—"

"Hah! You understand nothing. Nothing! And stop calling him an old geek. That term is about as dated as Lance Trainor!"

He let the cutting remark slide; he had never seen her so upset. "Is it money?" he asked gently.

She whipped around, eyes sizzling. Is that what he thought of her? That she couldn't get a man close to her own age, and wanted an old man for his money? A quid pro quo, so to speak—youth for money. Every time he opened his mouth, he dug the knife into her heart a little deeper.

"Yes, it's money," she spat, shoving his hand away. She glared at him. "Now, are you satisfied?

I don't happen to see myself living the rest of my life in a garret with a starving painter. Get out. You've found out what you came for."

Tears filled her eyes and her shoulders shook. She was coming apart, and she didn't want to give him the satisfaction of watching.

"Don't," he whispered, coming up behind her. "Please, don't." He placed his large hands on her shoulders, turning her into his arms. She would have pushed him away, but it felt too good. He placed his hand on her cheek, wiping away a tear with his thumb. "I'm sorry, little one. I guess I went a little crazy. I didn't want you to throw yourself at someone who doesn't deserve you."

Stunned, Holly knew something was about to happen when his hand slipped to the nape of her neck and drew her closer. She stared at him through tear-filled eyes. She knew she shouldn't let it happen, not while there was so much yet to be said, but she was helpless to stop it. She was emotionally drained. She had to kiss him; she had to torture herself with what might have been.

His lips touched her cheek, kissing away the tears, then he dropped a tender kiss on each eyelid, closing them against the world, folding her into his. He moved his mouth to cover her lips. This was her truth . . . this was where she wanted to be. The blood pounded in her head. With a low moan, she reached up to put her small hands around his neck, pulling him closer to her. The kiss went on until the anger left both their systems. And then it went on because neither of them could stop.

He lifted his head, gazing down at the woman he held in his arms. She clogged his senses. Her eyes were soft and honey-warm and utterly trusting. He felt like a first-class heel. He had swiftly reached a point where he wanted to take her into the bedroom.

He stroked her hair. "I just didn't want you to waste your youth on an old man. May and December unions rarely work."

"Is that why you kissed me?" she asked.

He smiled into her eyes. "I kissed you because I don't want to lose a friend."

It was easier to lose a friend than to lose a heart, she thought, closing the door after he left. She was in danger of losing both.

Holly touched her swollen lips. The back of her eyelids stung, and she fought the easy release of tears. Her heart was beating wildly. She had never expected Steven to kiss her. His last words to her didn't still the odd excitement rushing through her veins like a cascading waterfall.

If Steven kissed this way in friendship, what must it feel like to be in his arms and be kissed with the passion of a lover? Would a sexual relationship with him be one of driving desire, with him in total control, or would he treat a woman with tenderness, meeting her as an equal? She'd never know. Her writer's imagination was running away with her again. It was obvious the kiss hadn't affected him as much as it had her. For a moment, a fleeting second, when his eyes had gone darkly intense, she thought he, too, had been moved by the kiss. And then he had spoken, and she had realized he was just showing pity for her because he thought she was involved with an old geek.

Calming down, she realized she should be grateful for the mix-up. His assumption that she and Digger were having an affair was ludicrous, but lucky. But once again she had missed an opportunity to set the record straight. Until she was able to, her mission remained clear—she would still protect his home and his privacy while he was away.

She walked slowly back into the living room and slumped down wearily on the couch. When this assignment was over, she'd tackle a cookbook—it would be easier on her nerves.

Steven rode down on the elevator, deep in thought. He was frowning, trying to figure out what had possessed him to kiss Liz. He had certainly never meant for it to happen. Yet, at the time, it had seemed the most natural thing in the world.

He didn't want to think of her with that man. He hadn't seen him clearly, but he knew instinctively he wasn't for her. She needed someone who could devote time to her. Someone who wasn't averse to marriage. Someone free to marry, to give her babies.

She shouldn't be sneaking around with a married man. Oh, she had told him the man wasn't married, she had even said he wasn't her lover— but her face had been beet-red when she said it. He didn't believe her.

He kept thinking about the kiss on the drive back to his office. The truth was, it had knocked the socks off him. Liz was soft and eager and vulnerable. Too vulnerable. When she looked at him with tear-filled eyes, he couldn't stand it. It tore him apart to know his temper had been the cause of her distress.

So that, he decided after much deliberation, was why he had acted imprudently and kissed her. He had meant it as a friendly kiss, but he'd let it go on too long. Then he'd let his hands roam up her spine, fitting her womanly curves to his hips. He'd let his teeth nibble at her lower lip, he'd let himself taste the sweetness she had to offer. But it was for her own good—to show her she needed someone to light her fires, not bank them.

And why then did she return the kiss? he asked himself. *Because she's all mixed-up with her problems. Because you were there. Because you took advantage of a situation and forced yourself on her.*

The only thing he could do now to preserve their friendship was to get away from her for a while. If he didn't, she might get the idea that he was interested in trading his bachelor status for marriage. She'd been right when she had told him her private life was her own business. It was.

He looked forward to escaping to Oxnard, to fishing near the Channel Islands, maybe getting in a little snorkeling. Ginger could use the apartment. When he returned from his trip, he might even attend a few social functions—he was even pleasantly anticipating Marte Cudworth's party.

By the time he reached his office, he felt much better.

That night, a dozen long-stemmed-beauty roses arrived at the Mason apartment. The note to Liz read:

Liz,

Sorry for stepping out of line today. These roses are my way of saying I trust you to make the right decisions with your life. I'll be gone for about a week. We'll talk when I get back.

Steve,

Holly read and reread the note, focusing in on his second sentence. "I trust you to make the right decisions with your life." *Yes, I will, but at what cost?* she thought, sobbing into her pillow.

Six

Holly stepped onto the scale. She hadn't seen Steven all week. As she watched the needle shake and settle, she decided that being upset was excellent for the figure. In seven days she had shed five pounds. Her cheeks were becoming fashionably hollow, her hip bones were visible, and her tummy concave. She was beginning to look right at home in Beverly Hills—a shade anorexic, with a suntan!

Steven's note had challenged her to be true to herself. She had thought about it constantly in the ensuing days. She owed Steven loyalty, regardless of the fact that he was a blind fool who didn't return her love. One thing had nothing to do with the other.

She climbed the two flights of stairs to the penthouse. Since her frightening experience in the elevator, she thought twice before getting in it alone any more than she had to. With Steven, she didn't mind—he made her feel safe.

The two buckets she carried were filled with a complete assortment of household cleaning supplies. Never having been in his apartment, she didn't know what he needed. All she knew—thanks to Digger—was that Steven had paid a cool two million dollars, pre-construction price.

Her first impulse upon opening Steven's door was to turn and flee.

So was her second.

She realized now how cavalierly Steven had dismissed the size of his apartment, saying it was a bit larger than Mason's. If the room she was staring at were any indication of the rest of Steven's home, she might get lost!

One whole wall boasted a magnificent California stone fireplace. The rest of the walls were floor-to-ceiling windows that overlooked Wilshire Boulevard. Furniture groupings broke up the vast space to give it a feeling of intimacy. The furniture—what she could glimpse of it under the clutter—was mainly modern.

By nature an extremely neat person, Holly/Liz/Hortense shuddered at the thought of clutter. And she positively cringed at the idea of making order out of chaos. If this were only one room, what must the rest of the apartment look like? Her mother would say, "Consider it a challenge."

Clucking disapprovingly, she realized why anyone in his right mind *would* run away—or spend a lot of time in *her* apartment instead. No wonder Steven had attached himself to her . . . when he wasn't attaching himself to the blonde in his dreams!

She followed the trail of clutter into another large room—a game room. She carefully side-stepped a small electric practice putting green, a golf club, several golf balls, and a tennis racket. She stopped to examine his eclectic taste in art and bric-a-brac. Or were they priceless antiques?

How did one classify a merry-go-round horse, standing in one corner with a stuffed bear seated on it? Or a barber-shop Indian, tilted against a barber pole? Off to one corner of the cathedral-ceilinged room was a regulation-size billiard table, complete with a low-hanging Tiffany light fixture above it. A collection of cowboy hats hung on a wooden rack near framed portraits of—who else?—Lance Trainor! His home was typical of Steven. If she didn't know he was a successful businessman, she'd have thought he was a successful, grown-up kid.

Except, of course, when he kissed her. She still tingled when she thought about that. Only a man—a very experienced man—could make a woman go from steaming to sizzling in two seconds flat. She got goosebumps when she thought about it.

The amazing trail then led her to the dining room. There, on an oval-shaped banquet table, were twenty feathered hats and noisemakers, the remnants of a party that must have been a doozy. *When*, she wondered, *did Steven throw the party?* In her mind's eye she saw the magnificent room with its leaded crystal chandelier as it should be—

clean and sparkling. Fascinated, she continued her tour.

The more she saw, the more she was filled with annoyance. Setting herself up as Steven's guardian was one thing, but she needed help with this apartment.

She dialed Digger on a Mickey Mouse telephone. The thought of Steven barking orders to her over this phone made her smile. So how could she remain peeved with a man who talked on a Mickey Mouse phone, owned his own merry-go-round horse, munched caramel popcorn, and loved Lance Trainor so much he displayed the former cowboy's sweaty old hats prominently in his house?

"Digger," she said, hearing her boss's intimate Southern-tinged hello—the one he reserved only for people furnishing gossip.

"Oh, it's you. What do you want?" Digger switched to his snappy, New York office voice, the edges cutting.

"*I* don't want anything," Holly replied quickly, forcefully. Her eyes steamrolled over piles of litter. "Hortense does. Hortense needs a maid."

Holly held the receiver away from her ear. The expected barrage began in exactly two seconds. "What do you mean, Hortense needs a maid? Hortense *is* a maid! Stop wasting my time, Holly. My editor's hounding me for the last chapter. Am I supposed to inform her I'm waiting for you to find me some juicy details? All the stuff you've given me these past two weeks is worthless. Who cares if Chadwick's clean-living?"

Holly bit her lower lip to keep from screaming at

Digger about his misplaced values. One of the things she admired about Steven was his penchant for clean living—immediate surroundings excluded, of course.

"Think of the times we live in, Digger," she said.

He cut her off, adroitly avoiding her meaning. "Precisely. What woman wants to sit through boring westerns starring an old silent picture star? Believe me, after the oatmeal pap you've told me about Chadwick, I'd switch bachelors if I could, but it's too late. I did too good a job selling him to my editor. You mentioned he was seeing Louise Armand. Get me some dirt on that angle."

"I made a mistake. He isn't dating her." Why did she feel as if she had to protect Louise too?

"No problem. I'll say he just broke up with her and is looking for the woman of his dreams. Better for the book."

She was appalled at how Digger fabricated stories. With his every word, Digger unwittingly convinced her she was doing the right thing in shielding Steven from his clutches.

"Does this mean Hortense doesn't get a maid?"

Digger's New York accent zinged over the line. "Bingo. You've hit the jackpot."

The connection went dead.

Resigned to her formidable task, Holly picked up a dustcloth and went to work. She went into one of the two rooms she hadn't seen yet and let out a soft gasp. His study was spotless, orderly, beautiful. A sense of peace permeated the well-used room. The huge oak desk gleamed with a rich patina. Near a wall of windows overlooking the posh area, she saw his drafting table, a rack holding his blueprints, a plotting table, and his computer. Shelves of books lined another wall. Examining the spines, she noted that only a portion of the books were devoted to his field of architecture. The rest were eclectic—running the gamut from art to spy thrillers to economics and philosophy—and all were well-worn.

He was a man, she learned, who liked to surround himself with mementos. Hanging behind his desk was a framed letter signed by the President, praising him for the home his company had designed, built, and donated to house unwed mothers in Chicago.

Awed, Holly studied the contents of the room, learning more about this complex man whom she loved. There was a gilt-framed picture of Louise. Surprisingly, there were several miniature oil portraits; one in particular caught her eye. She lingered over it, studying its delicate composition of a young woman with flowing, golden hair. Although the subject was viewed only from the back, the sense of movement, the feel of the wind lilting her hair, the action of her arms and legs, all contributed to motion. Instinctively, Holly knew that if the young woman turned around, she'd be beautiful.

She peered closer to read the talented artist's name. Tugged by an invisible force, she checked the others. All bore his initials: S.W.C. She couldn't believe it. Steven was an artist too!

For the next two hours she cleaned and picked

up his discarded clothes, but instead of resenting it, her mind was carefully sorting out this new picture of him.

She hadn't yet set foot inside his bedroom; she was feeling shy about seeing the bed in which he slept. And, like a sweet confection, she was saving the best for last.

The huge bed draped in brown satin sheets was set on a raised pedestal in the center of the room. The ceiling above it was a massive, dome-shaped skylight. A light touch on a button by the bed drew the glass panels back to allow fresh breezes in and the twinkling stars to shine as a romantic canopy.

All her warm, new, respectful feelings toward Steven flew out the window as a fit of jealousy overtook her. Had she first examined the down pillows with the telltale strands of blond hair mixed with the dark ones, she never would have bothered to pick up any of his mess! As it was, she was sorely tempted to throw a few things back onto the Aubusson rug.

Not that Rasputin the Renaissance man would notice. This hair belonged, no doubt, to the blonde he had been dreaming about while *she* was mustering up enough courage to continue with her confession! The blonde of the miniature painting perhaps? . . .

Holly distastefully plucked the hairs from the pillow. Poor Louise. If she and Steven really were lovers, then he was two-timing her. For the first time, Holly felt a twinge of pity for the hard-working actress. The telltale dark hairs on one pillow were the same shade as Steven's; the telltale blond hairs on the other pillow were the same shade as her own. She knew damn well *she* hadn't been sleeping with him. Louise, a true redhead, hadn't been in that bed lately either. Was it possible Steven and Louise really *were* friends, and nothing more?

And if that were true—so what? It didn't leave much room for her. The evidence was clear—blond hairs twining with dark hairs was proof enough.

A bit of peach-colored lace froth at the foot of the bed caught her eye. She picked it up, confirming her suspicion. Louise couldn't possibly fit her statuesque figure into the itty-bitty excuse for a nightie.

In the interest of research, she held it in her hand to try and calculate its weight, rubbing her fingers over the transparent material. Two ounces, tops! She examined the postage-stamp-sized material. Somehow, she found herself in front of the beveled mirror, holding it against her body.

She quickly stripped, overwhelmed by a sudden curiosity to see how she'd look in the kind of clothes Steven preferred in a woman. She unpinned the clasp holding her thick hair; it fell like a shining cascade to frame her shoulders. The gossamer-silk gown slid over her body, molding itself to her curves. The delicate lingerie exposed her breasts and shape in a way that was sexier than being naked. This gown, she realized as she pirouetted in front of the mirror, wasn't designed for a woman to sleep alone in. It promised pleasure, the texture of a lover's hands urgent with need—a lover who would toss it quickly to the end of the bed. Is that, she wondered miserably, what he had done?

She shook her head to clear her impossible thoughts. After all, Steven and his blonde were two consenting adults in the privacy of their own home.

She removed the diaphanous wisp of clothing. The lingering kiss of silk on her body was a new and wonderful sensation. Nothing at all like the mother hubbard nightgown Steven had seen her in the night they'd met. All that showed were her toes! It was no wonder he looked at her like a sister and kissed her in friendship.

A black dress lay across a brown velvet chair—if one could call the backless and frontless item a dress, she thought, picking it up to examine it. No store she knew of in Minneapolis carried one like it. Assuring herself it was all in the interests of research, she slipped into it.

A miracle of two wafer-thin straps held it together. The dress, slashed in a deep vee down the front, was designed to be worn minus a bra. As she modeled in front of the mirror, she decided the only thing holding it up was hope.

She slipped back into her own clothes, clothes that couldn't hold a candle to the ones worn by Steven's ladylove. With an increasingly heavy heart, she thought of what she had learned. Steven was a complex, caring, intelligent man—who also played the field!

She had learned something about herself too. First and foremost, she was determined to know who the mystery woman in his life was. Not for

Digger—for herself! She had also discovered she liked the ultra-feminine clothes the woman wore.

The gold mantle clock chimed four bells. Exhausted from all her hard work, Holly gave one satisfied look around. His apartment was spotless. Fresh linens were on the bed, and it was covered with a patterned comforter. The mystery woman's clothes were hung up in the closet. What would it be like, she thought fleetingly, if it were her blond hair on the pillow instead of someone else's?

At the last minute she impishly wrote Steven a note.

Dear Mr. Chadwick,
   It took me far longer to clean your apartment than anticipated. This was due to clothes left on the bed, remnants of a party, and general litter. I really have to be able to see the floors and the furniture in order to clean. I'm sure you will understand why I've had to re-compute the bill.

                                        Hortense

When Steven arrived home days later he found his apartment meticulously clean; he also found the note. He was hopping mad at his sister Ginger. Impatiently, he strummed his fingers while waiting for her to answer the phone. On the eighth ring, she picked it up.

"I'm going to dispense with the niceties, Ginger, since it's obvious you dispensed with them when you borrowed my home."

She capitulated immediately. "Sorry!"

He simmered with rage. "Young lady, what the hell went on here? You told me you needed a place to crash, not trash. According to my new maid, that's exactly what you did here. She wrote me a note to the effect that I trashed the place with a lady friend. Now, who the hell was here and what the hell happened?"

"Steve, I'm truly sorry," she apologized. "Fran and I couldn't resist sleeping in your bed, what with the skylight and all. We woke up late and had to be at school for an early morning class. I guess I left some of my clothes on your bed. Sorry. When I'm in the neighborhood, I'll pick them up. Not to worry, big brother."

He raked his fingers through his hair. Fatigue lined his face; he was dead-tired from his trip. It had gone well, and finally the snafu in Santos had been cleared up. Larry had joined him on the latter part of his trip.

"Okay," he decided wearily. "You're on probation, squirt. By the way, tell Mom I'm sending her the merry-go-round horse for her charity affair. There's a little something extra sitting on it. I think the kids in the hospital will get a kick out of it."

"Gee, I almost forgot. Mom asked if she could borrow the miniature oil painting you did of me. She only needs it for a short while."

"Fine. I'll have everything shipped by one of my trucks." He said good-bye quickly.

He wanted a shower and bed. In that order. He picked up his jacket from the chair and hung it in the closet. Hortense, he realized, could easily become a pain in the neck. But where in hell was he going to find a maid who cleaned as well?

Exhausted, he flopped down on his bed. His tie was askew, his shirt was unbuttoned, his shoes were off—put away neatly in his closet. With Hortense's note still in his hand, he dialed Louise. Her first words to him told him she was expecting Larry to call.

"Save the sexy hello for someone who appreciates it."

"Phooey. What did you call for, Snookums?"

He rolled his eyes heavenward. "I called to tell you your college-bound Hortense laid down the law—part of which you deserve. So here goes. Unless you provide cleanup for these little shindigs you keep throwing for Larry—my place is off limits."

Louise made a sound of appreciation, surprising him. "Good for Hortense. I dare say, you seem to have found two of the women already. Except Hortense is old enough to be your mother. How do you feel about older women?"

"What are you talking about?" he asked, puzzled.

"Don't you remember? I told you that in order for you to be happy, you'd have to find three women—"

"May I remind you, were I contemplating marriage—which I'm not—there's a law forbidding bigamy in this state."

Louise was undaunted. "Well, how about the other one?"

"What other one?"

"Oh, for goodness' sake, it's Miss what's-her-name."

He knew Louise was fully aware of Liz's name. "What has Liz to do with your fruity ideas?"

Louise sounded exasperated. "For a smart man, you're pretty dumb. In case you haven't noticed, your ulcer symptoms disappeared with the appearance of Liz Mason. You've even gotten friendlier."

"I like being a bachelor. It keeps me out of trouble."

"Why don't you ask Liz to Marte Cudworth's party? And don't tell me you aren't going. Marte already told me you are."

"Don't change the subject. You have your own place. Why haven't you been using it?"

"Darling," she purred, demonstrating with her sexy tones why the movie-going public adored her, "Larry doesn't approve of my house. Can I help it if it's built on the San Andreas fault? He says if we make love on my bed, we could start an earthquake. I say, if it was once good enough for Errol Flynn, it's good enough for me. I'm making progress though," Louise boasted, "even without your help. The other day I burned his toast. He said I'm finally learning to cook the way his mother does. Isn't that wonderful?"

Steven closed his eyes. Tucking the receiver under his jaw, he let his hand flop down. "How do you change the subject like that? It's wonderful. I'm changing the locks. Good night."

Turning his cheek on the pillow, he yawned.

The faint scent of jasmine wafted into his nostrils. Images of Liz flitted through his mind. Her taste was still on his lips. He had spent the week waffling, keeping his hand away from the telephone. Liz was not the kind of woman to play fast and loose. She was the marrying kind. The for-keeps, till-death-do-us-part, forever-after kind. All the things a confirmed bachelor like himself shied away from.

Seven

Holly finished kneading the dough for the Irish soda bread she was making for her brother Mark. It was his favorite. She had been so happy when she'd received his call telling her he was visiting Los Angeles to attend a meeting of the Bar Association. Now she wasn't sorry that he was staying at a hotel instead of accepting her offer to spend the weekend with her. The visit had gotten off to a rocky start.

Spooning the raisin-dotted mixture into a round pan, she placed it in the oven and set the timer. They were in the middle of a rare dispute. Washing her hands, she turned to gesture. In doing so, she knocked over a bottle of soda onto the tiled floor. Cursing inwardly, she tore off several sheets of paper toweling from the Lucite towel holder and bent down to wipe up the puddle.

"Mark, I'm a grown woman. I resent this third-degree grilling."

Mark's golden coloring and hers were similar. Friends of their family always marveled at the closeness between the two. They'd be given one heck of an earful now, she thought ruefully.

He leaned against the work island in the center of the modern kitchen. "What you are doing is the most preposterous crap I've ever heard! And besides," he warned with the acute perception of a prosecuting attorney, "did you ever think you could be arrested for breaking and entering?"

"I am not breaking and entering," she protested. "I have the key."

She got up and went to a small drawer near the telephone. She extracted a key and thrust it under his nose. "See!" Returning the key to the drawer, she bent down again to finish what she had started.

"I'm not impressed," Mark scoffed. "When Digger uses the material for his own personal gain, the charge won't matter. It spells trouble."

Holly paused. She rocked back on her heels, pressing her hands on her knees. "You haven't been listening!" Holly cried passionately. "You and Digger are like bookends. You're both squeezing me! He's insinuating that I'm dragging my feet on purpose so I can cozy up to Steven for personal profit. You're telling me that I'm probably going to be sued!" Her eyes sizzled with indignation. "As a matter of fact, I'm doing Steven a favor. I'm cleaning his apartment while I'm looking out for his interests. Anyhow, once I tell Steven about Digger, he's free to do whatever he wants."

Mark gestured helplessly. "So—you came west to become a maid and a glorified version of Robin Hood! What's happening to you? You were always such a sensible girl. We always knew where we stood with you."

"Maybe I'm tired of having people always know where they stand with me!" she said. Being taken for granted was the story of her life. Well, she'd just wrote the last chapter on that nonsense!

Mark continued. "When you left home to come to this—this—"

"Den of depravity," she supplied acidly.

"Exactly." Mark met her tone. "We expected you to get a by-line in a magazine, to meet interesting people, and—"

Bristling, she cocked her head to stifle his accusation. "I *am* meeting interesting people," she flared. "You don't think I spend every waking moment on Steven's case, do you? I've interviewed others, and written articles too." She balled the wet paper towel in her hand.

Mark crouched down on his knees, leveling his charge straight at her. "Holly, I swear I don't know what to make of you. Why the hell are you really doing this?"

She wanted to wallop him. "I told you why. I'm doing it to protect Steven."

"Protect him by telling him the truth!"

"I tried to, dammit!"

"Well, what happened?"

"He fell asleep."

"He *what*?"

She knew it sounded ridiculous. But it was

true. "You heard me. And before you make any wise remarks, I tried more than once to tell Steven what was going on. Something always seemed to happen. It's like a curse."

Seeing her obviously agitated state, Mark eased his tone. "Tell me about it," he urged.

"You had to be there to know what went on. Steven is really a very nice man. Look how nice and friendly he's been to me." Her expression dared her brother to disagree. "Oh, I know he can act nutty, but he cares about people, especially the people who work for him. He's been so worried about business. I didn't have the heart to add to his woes." She wiped a damp lock of hair from her forehead. "I mean, how would you feel if your company stood to lose millions of dollars? All because of an unfair moratorium after all the work had been approved. Bad, right?"

She didn't wait for an answer, but rushed on. "And wouldn't you feel badly about the workers in the field whom you know don't have bank accounts large enough to carry them through? Some of them even moved their families from other cities because the construction would take so long."

Mark put his hand on her shoulder. "Slow down, Holly, you're rambling."

"It was a judgment choice," she explained. "Upset Steven or protect him a little while longer."

"So you decided to protect him?" It was clear Mark still wasn't sure how all this led up to her being a maid.

Holly nodded. She tossed the wet toweling into the garbage pail and rose. "Then he went out of town. That's where he is now. Actually, he didn't go alone. His lawyer went with him. Larry's in love with Louise."

Mark uttered an oath. "Holly, what's gotten into you? I can't make head or tail out of this. Will you please just stick to the facts!"

"I'm trying. Pay attention! Steven's trying to salvage something out of this mess, mostly for the men. He says his lifestyle won't change because of the loss."

"I'm certainly glad to hear that."

Holly bristled. "Don't be sarcastic."

"Never mind, I get the general idea. Go on."

Holly was only too glad not to elaborate on more than was necessary. She heaved a sigh. "So you see, if I don't pretend to be the maid until this is cleared up, Digger will hire someone who really *will* snoop. You don't know what he's like. He sends out operatives all the time."

"Operatives!" Mark threw up his hands. "You sound as if you've been recruited by the CIA. If you go back up to Chadwick's apartment as . . . as . . . what's her name?" He inclined his head.

"Hortense Shaw."

Mark looked aghast. He banged his fist on the butcher-block counter top, sending flour spraying upward. "With all due respect to your good intentions, I'm a lawyer, sis. I'm an officer of the court. I took an oath to uphold the laws of the court."

She felt frazzled. She'd explained everything; it was quite clear in her mind. Her ears hurt from listening to Mark's objections.

"Am I stopping you? Go home. Uphold the laws

of the court. Run for office. Uphold anything you want, but get off my case." She blew another strand of hair from the corner of her mouth, and flounced past him into the living room, halting in front of the coffee table. Steven's biography was spread out near his picture, along with the notes she'd prepared for Digger in case Steven agreed to be interviewed. Even recalling his mussed-up bed— the one with the blond hairs on the pillow— Steven's picture pulled at her heart. He looked so dear, and she wanted him so much. Why couldn't she be a femme fatale instead of a popcorn buddy?

Mark trailed after her into the room. She blinked back a mist of frustrated tears. "I hoped you'd see what I've been doing as a rare opportunity to meet interesting people."

She was interrupted by a snort of derision. "So who have you met? Tell me that, will you? Apart from filtering through his garbage—"

She cut him off, speaking sharply. "I never did that!"

"Okay, you and I don't see eye to eye on this thing. If I were licensed in this state, I'd take his case. Gratis. Because, believe me, when your little Robin-Hood scheme gets out, you're going to be in trouble!" His jaw held the determined look of a buffalo about to charge. "When a person sues, he sues up the line. Everybody." He pointed his finger accusingly at her.

Holly was no stranger to her brother's knowledge of the law. He had made Law Review in his second year, and was a cum laude graduate. Now he worked for a major law firm in Minneapolis. If *he* was worried she'd be sued, then there was a strong possibility Steven might do just that. She'd seen Steven angry, knew his temper if pushed.

Gloomily, she pictured the tableau in the courtroom. She'd be represented by a court-appointed counsel—trying his first case—as befitted her empty pocketbook. Steven would be surrounded by a battery of high-priced lawyers. He'd be dressed like his idol Lance Trainor, complete with a dusty Stetson and side arms slung low around his narrow hips. He'd stomp over in his trail-worn cowboy boots to where she sat huddled with her neophyte attorney—the one who had flunked the bar on his first two attempts. Steven would scrunch up his blue eyes into vindictive, narrow slits, aimed at her—like squinting over the barrel of a rifle! His lovely, sensuous mouth would be drawn into a thin, grim, furious line. Even his eyebrows would be one black, condemning brushstroke.

And she rebelled. At Steven *and* at Mark. How dare Steven treat her like that! How dare Mark have no faith in her!

"You're just like Steven. He's always bossing me too. What is it with you men? Do I look like someone to be trampled on? Can't you conduct a simple conversation without pointing and shouting?" she shouted. She was so distraught she didn't see the expression on her brother's face change from a scowl to one of amazed curiosity.

"Tell me something, sis," Mark asked carefully. "How often does this Chadwick boss you?"

"His name is Steven," she mumbled. It was foolish to fight with Mark, she knew. It was just that his logic frustrated her so much. After Steven learned the truth, if he didn't appreciate her noble motives, she'd need every friend she could get. *Mea culpa.* She'd throw herself on the mercy of the court!

"How often?" Mark prompted, keeping his voice calm.

She sighed and closed her eyes, reliving the times she and Steven had been together. "It depends on your definition of bossing, I suppose. Counting the guggle muggle . . . his jogging program that he wants me to join . . . his nudging me to find Lance Trainor—"

"The old-time cowboy star?"

"Mmmm, yes. Steven has a thing about him. Well, counting all that, plus insisting that I learn how to fish. . . ."

Incredulous, Mark dropped a picture of Steven he had held up to examine. "But you hate fishing!"

"It's a long story," she sighed, avoiding Mark's gaze in her misery. She knew his outburst was due to concern for her. "Anyway, what difference does it make? I've lost count."

A beginning of a smile tugged at the corners of Mark's handsome mouth. Tall, with blond, wavy hair, he was one of those rare persons who seemed to have everything. Looks, charm, and brains—the latter of which he was using now.

"What's a guggle muggle?" he asked gently, watching her.

"Poison. Hot milk, butter, honey, and rum. He made me drink it to cure a cold."

Mark made a sympathetic face. "And did it cure you?"

"Yes," she admitted reluctantly.

The lawyer in him probed deeper. "You say he's designing an exercise program for you?"

"Yes," she remarked with a wistful smile. Steven looked so good in his jogging shorts. "Until I met him, my life was simple."

"And boring." He reminded her of her own reason for leaving home, then studied her in speculative silence for a few more moments. "How often does he come around?"

Holly leaned back on the sofa, removing her glasses. She dangled one of the frame's end pieces in her mouth, concentrating.

"When he's home . . . I'd say once a day."

Her brother's eyebrows formed a question. "Are you two dating?" he asked quickly.

"No," Holly instantly shot back. "You might say he feels responsible for me. I'm more like his mascot."

"Mascot?" Mark sounded surprised.

"Yes, I think he was a Saint Bernard in another life. Or an Indian."

Thoroughly confused, but keeping his growing suspicions to himself, he paraphrased her words. "Comes around every day, huh?"

She nodded, avoiding Mark's keen gaze. She wasn't about to recount the scene in the elevator with Steven. Nor was she about to tell him that Steven had kissed her—even in friendship. Nor did she feel like talking about Louise. The truth was, every time she thought about Louise, she saw red. Then she saw green, wondering about the sexy blonde who had left her calling card on his pillow!

Mark gazed intently at his sister. For the first time since their conversation began, he looked relieved. "I think I made a mistake. Chadwick might let you off the hook, but he'll hang Digger."

"How do you know that?"

He curled a lock of her glowing, golden hair around his finger. "The birds and the bees."

Holly briefly considered telling Mark he was crazy, then thought better of it. "You're not making any sense."

He chuckled. "Neither are you. Do you really think he's coming around every day to check up on you out of a sense of duty? Boy Scouts help old women across the street out of a sense of duty. Busy architects don't plan exercise programs, bring in popcorn, share favorite movies—and what else did you say? Suggest an outing on the briny blue— out of a sense of duty. I've got to hand it to you, Holly; when you break out, you really break out," he said admiringly.

Holly wasn't sure what Mark was getting at, but she was glad her fight with her brother was over.

Apparently, so was he. "Why don't we forget about all this and go out on the town? You can show me the sights, and we'll plan a wonderful day for tomorrow."

"I'd love it. What would you like to see? The cultural sights—"

"No," he interrupted. "How about going where we're liable to see some movie stars?"

She wouldn't mind a diversion either. "There's a nightclub called La Mama's. It's very exclusive."

"Can we get in?"

"I'll phone for reservations. This is one time it pays to work for Digger."

They were interrupted suddenly by the ringing of the doorbell.

"Speak of the devil," Mark said. "Could that be Digger?"

An all-too-familiar voice called out, settling the owner's identity. "Open up. It's Steve. I'm back."

Holly dropped her glasses. *Not again. He can't be back! The timing is all wrong!*

"Ohmygosh!" she whispered, sending a shocked look to her brother.

"The plot thickens," he whispered back.

"Hey, open up, Liz! I know you're home. I can hear you in there."

How dare he always pop in on her? He expected her to be at his beck and call!

"Just a second, Steven." She had to send him away. She didn't want him seeing Mark—there'd be too many questions. When she spoke to Steven, she wanted to control the situation, not the other way around.

"Liz?" Mark put a restraining hand on her arm as she made a mad dash back to the coffee table to clear off its telltale contents. "Did I miss something before? Who's Liz? I thought you were parading around as Hortense. Are there three of you?"

She glanced anxiously at him. This was a time for faith. She just knew trouble was coming.

"Please, don't ask questions. I'm all three, but Steven only knows me as Liz Mason."

"Mason? You mean the guy who owns this place?" When she nodded, Mark's tone dropped a censorious octave. "You're using your middle name and someone else's last name!" He let out a low whistle. "I've changed my mind again. Chadwick doesn't need protection, you do." He stared at Holly in amazement, scratching his head as if he had just stepped onto a Groucho Marx movie set.

"Mark," she begged, "I told you it was complicated. Trust me. This is all for Steven's own good."

"Deliver me from ever letting you do something for my own good! This gets better by the minute." He couldn't help chuckling. "When are you going to let him in? He sounds impatient."

"He's always impatient," she said, thinking fast. Mark wasn't her immediate problem—Steven was. She dashed into the bedroom for her trusty trash bag. While her brother watched with an incredulous stare on his face, she took her arm and swept everything from the coffee table into the garbage bag. Then she hurried again toward the bedroom.

She turned back. "Let him in," she whispered, realizing she'd have to change and see Steven after all. Her eyes implored Mark to cover for her. "Introduce yourself; I've got to change my clothes. And please,"—she dashed back to wring her brother's hand—"don't act surprised when you see me. I'm not going to look the same. Just go along with anything I say. And whatever you do, *don't* call me Holly!"

"Are you going to tell him about Digger?"

"Yes," she promised. "But not right now, not with you here. It wouldn't be right. Would it?"

"No, I guess not. The guy deserves some privacy," Mark agreed.

The doorbell rang again.

She breathed a sigh of relief. Mark, thank goodness, would keep quiet—temporarily!

"Just a second!" She remembered their relationship. She ran back to her brother, stopping him from opening the door at the last second. She yanked him away.

"Don't tell him you're my brother. If you do, he'll want to know why we have different last names. He's a very suspicious person by nature," she hissed, thinking back to the time Steven had seen her with Digger and mistaken him for her aging lover. "I'll clear the whole thing up later. Let him think you're my date."

"This is a three-ring circus. Go ahead—Liz, Hortense, Holly," he said expansively. His hand was on the doorknob. "I promise to go along with whatever you say. In fact, I can't wait to see what happens. Boy, am I glad I came to California. You were right, sis; there's plenty of excitement out here. Heck—I may even move out here myself!"

Eight

Holly spent the next few minutes in the bathroom, washing and forcing herself to calm down. Then she began her metamorphosis into Liz. From the living room, she heard murmurs and snatches of conversation, then raucous laughter. "Good," she said aloud. "That's one less thing to worry about." Still, she wished she could be a fly on the wall to make certain her brother was keeping his word.

It's too late now anyway, she admitted, giving in to a feeling of paralysis. *Whatever will be, will be.* She'd done all she could for Steven. And in the process, she had fallen in love.

During the week she had returned to her apartment for more clothes, but, remembering the sensuous silk against her skin, she had purchased a copy of *Vogue*, studying the fashion styles carefully. By Beverly Hills standards, she knew she still didn't measure up.

Yesterday, she had driven over to Robinson's in the Valley, where she'd splurged on a designer-label dress in a fabulous pink silk fabric. She couldn't resist it because, when she had tried it on, the dress fit as if it were made especially for her. It hugged her narrow rib cage, showing off her breasts, and clung sensuously around her hips, her softly rounded curves, and well-shaped legs. Her blond hair sparkled against the pale-pink material.

With the dress on and makeup and wig in place, she opened the small container with the contact lenses and put one in each eye. The effect was worth it. Her eyes looked different, more glamorous.

With a last check in the mirror, she took a deep breath. Holding her head high, she joined the men. Steven probably wouldn't notice whether she wore a dress or a suit, or even that she wasn't wearing her tortoiseshell glasses.

She was wrong. He noticed—immediately. He let out an audible gasp of pleasure. He couldn't take his eyes off her. And Mark noticed Steven noticing. And grinned.

Holly blushed furiously. Her brother's Cheshire-cat grin was slapped all over his puss.

Steven cut off his words to Mark in midsentence. He drew in a soft breath. "Liz, you look lovely."

"*Mmmm.* I love your hair." Mark commented teasingly, standing next to Steven.

Holly groaned inwardly. Her brother was taking pleasure in her discomfort. Pointedly ignoring his double meaning, she held out her hand, speaking formally.

"Steven, you're back early. How nice to see you." That was an understatement! She couldn't take her eyes off him. If she stayed near him much longer, she wouldn't be responsible for her actions. He looked so handsome—dressed in blue slacks, a striped shirt, and navy blue blazer—that her pulse started racing. He was actually staring at her as if he'd never seen her before, and she wanted to kiss the surprise from his lips.

Forcing herself to speak in normal tones and not let him know the effect he was having on her heartbeat, Holly said, "I see you and Mark have already introduced yourselves. I'm so sorry." Her smile was hesitant. "You'll have to excuse us; we were just on our way out for the evening."

Steven took her statement in stride, paying no attention to her announcement. She was shocked when he came over and gathered her close to his side. He draped his arm casually around her shoulder, letting his fingers unconsciously rub the bare flesh beneath the hem of her sleeve. The touch of Steven's hand on her skin brought the usual response—her body felt as if it were electrically charged! His fingers ran lightly up over her shoulder to rest at the base of her neck. He was listening to something Mark was saying while turning erotic circles with his thumb. It was all she could do to refrain from moaning.

Steven looked down at her, smiling. "I understand you're planning on hitting some of the high spots tonight. I can't let you tool around in your tiny car when mine's gassed up and ready. How would you two like me to be your chauffeur?"

Mark accepted with alacrity, slapping his thigh. "We'd love it."

Holly glared at Mark. Steven beamed at them both. "Wonderful—then it's all set. We'll take the Mercedes; I don't think the three of us would be comfortable in the Ferrari."

Holly remained speechless and just continued to glare. Steven was at it again, showing his true bossy colors. Mark's lips were twitching.

And how, she wondered, had Steven managed to usurp their plans so smoothly? Why was her brother tugging at his jaw, containing the laughter she knew was hidden right below the surface? She could almost hear him say "Touché."

Then it dawned on her. Her brother, the traitorous louse, was in cahoots with Steven, without Steven even knowing it!

Steven wasn't finished yet; he had one more surprise up his sleeve. "Excuse us a minute, please, will you, Mark?" she heard him say, "Liz and I have some unfinished business to attend to." His hand beneath her elbow propelled her into the bedroom.

Neither one heard Mark say, "Go right ahead, kids, don't mind me."

"What unfinished business?" she protested the minute they were alone. She heard the lock on her door click into place.

The smile on Steven's face vanished, replaced

by a swift and accusing change in his demeanor. "I can't leave you alone for a minute, can I?"

She recoiled as if she had been slapped. "What?" She didn't know what she had been expecting, but it hadn't been to be insulted.

"Where did you pick him up?" He jerked his thumb toward the door. "What happened to the old geek?"

How dare he assume such a proprietary role with her? Here she had been thinking such loving thoughts, and they were all wasted.

"Stop using that word!" She glared at him and her chin came up. No man was going to boss her, ever again. Starting with Steven William Chadwick. She owed him nothing more than a certain degree of loyalty for being so nice to her in the elevator. That was all!

"Do you realize what you've done?" she fumed, stomping past him. The words tumbled out in a torrent. "You've manipulated my plans to suit you. You can't just horn in on my life!"

He gave her a look that clearly showed he didn't think much of her plans. "Don't be a fool. I'm only looking out for your welfare." His eyes narrowed thoughtfully. "How long have you known him?"

"All my life."

"What did you do with your glasses?"

"I'm wearing contacts. And it's none of your business anyway." She turned to order him to leave, but he was already beside her, slipping his arms around her.

He was looking at her with yearning. "Your eyes are all sparkly and dewy and—forget it," he muttered.

Sparkly and dewy. Holly felt a wild thrill ripple through her. Maybe she *had* inferred too much about Steven's relationship with Louise. After all, he wasn't married, and he insisted that Louise and Larry were an item. She just hadn't believed it, she was so jealous. If she had wanted to look at it rationally, the blond hairs on the pillow proved he was an unattached bachelor with healthy, normal urges.

And now—miracle of miracles!—Steven was finally seeing her as a woman. The tables were turned. *He* was jealous. Oh, it was a delicious feeling! Maybe he didn't know the real Holly yet, but she was just finding out the real Holly too. Maybe they could find out together?

It was a beginning.

She wanted to hug herself. Better yet, she wanted to hug *him.* For some incredible reason, Steven *was* jealous. This lovely man who smelled of musk and soap and whose summer-blue eyes made her all mushy inside was acting as if she were important to him.

She snuggled in his arms. He wouldn't sue her; she knew it with every melting bone in her body. She smiled coyly, lifting her lashes. "I've known Mark as long as you've known Louise, maybe longer," she repeated.

Steven stopped nuzzling her ear. He lifted his head, his lips thinned to a grimace. "He's from Minneapolis, then?"

She smiled. "Yes."

His fingers tightened on her waist. He lifted his brow. "He's not right for you."

She suppressed a joyous laugh. Steven looked so grim, like a man being led slowly, torturously away from confirmed bachelorhood. But she had to do it carefully, tenderly, so he wouldn't get spooked. Who knew better than she how he valued his single state?

Holly remembered every word her brother had said. *Boy Scouts help little old ladies across the street.* She wasn't a little old lady, and Steven was no Boy Scout. He was coming on to her like a jealous lover. Why? She didn't know, but whatever the reason, she decided to take advantage of a golden opportunity.

She tried to imagine what Louise might do in a similar situation. She could almost hear her sexy tones advising, "Go for it, honey."

Striving to sound nonchalant, Holly mimicked Steven's last comment. She swept her long lashes upward. "Not good for me, huh?"

He looked tense. "No," he clipped. "He's nice enough, but he's not the man for you."

Tell me you're the man for me, you big dope! She bit her quivering bottom lip. The man she wanted was standing right in front of her, too blind to see what was happening. He needed a little push—maybe a big one. She couldn't resist the heady sense of her own sexuality.

I've got to tell him the truth. "I quite agree," she said, feigning a serious demeanor. "Mark's my brother."

"Your brother!" He looked stunned.

Open your eyes, you fool, she silently implored.

Look at me, loving you. "Did you have anyone in mind you *would* approve of?"

Steven captured her face in his hand to examine her carefully. Her brother! That left the field wide open for him! What was he thinking? He was a confirmed bachelor! *Slow down,* he warned himself. He heard the minister ask, "Do you take this woman to be . . ."

He cleared his throat. "Liz, a man would be a fool not to appreciate your nice qualities—"

Stunned, she whirled away, tossing her head and not caring if the damned wig flew into his face. He was so pigheaded blind, she wanted to fry him for bacon! Nice qualities, indeed! It sounded as if he were pitching her as a warm coat. Serviceable, with good qualities. Last more than one season, folks. Hell, with any luck, she'd be discounted!

"I suppose you have an available list of qualified applicants," she said, furious he couldn't see beyond the nose on his stupidly gorgeous face!

"Oh, come on, now." He reached for her, but she pushed him away. Every time she thought she was making headway, why did he say something to kill it?

She spoke up sharply. "The next thing you'll dream up is that I need lessons in—"

Steven chuckled. She really was a delightful minx. "On second thought,"—his voice was low and teasingly intimate—"you could use a few lessons."

She bristled and placed her hands on her hips. "I could use a few lessons," she repeated, wondering what advice Louise would give in this situation. "In what?"

He hauled her back against him, squashing her arms to her sides. From the moment he had walked into the apartment tonight, seeing her dressed like a sexy siren, he had recognized an ache in his loins that had nothing to do with friendship. He ran his hands up her arms and over her shoulders, walking the fingertips to her collarbone, and upward to cup her face between his hands. He grinned.

"Why don't we start your lessons with kissing? Seems to me I remember you held back. Of course, that was understandable. We were only kissing in friendship, but if you want to land the right man, you've got to do better."

"You want to give me lessons in kissing, to catch a man! Is that it?" she asked, stunned at his audacity.

Steven didn't care how she put it. All he wanted to do was bury himself in her lips. The best antidote to a woman who drove his senses to the breaking point was to deal with her head-on—without making a lifetime commitment.

At that moment, Holly was sorely tempted to throw him to Digger and let the women of America tear into him. It would be no less than he deserved. With supreme effort, she forced herself to meet his gaze without flinching; keeping a tight rein on her control, she took a step backward.

Her voice almost cracked. "Let me get this straight. You want to make me over into the ideal woman—a woman who pleases a man by knowing how to kiss, jog, watch cowboy movies, eat caramel popcorn, and drink guggle muggles. Then I'd be perfect?"

Intoxicated by the scent of her, he stepped forward, closing the distance between them. "There's a little more to it than that. *Mmmm*, you smell nice. What are you wearing?"

"Jasmine," she said distractedly.

He knew then that, wherever he would be in the world again, the aroma of jasmine would always remind him of her. "I missed you," he murmured, rubbing his lips on her forehead. "I headed straight back to you to tell you we won in Santos. It's going to work out—the courts are making exceptions in certain cases. Seems we not only were in compliance with all the statutes, but we were able to prove hardship for everyone involved. That's quite a load off my mind. Why don't we celebrate?"

She didn't want to hear about it. Right now she didn't give a damn if his whole project slid right into the sea. She tilted her head. "And you took it for granted that I'd be home on a Saturday night, doing nothing in particular? Is that it?"

Steven gazed deeply into her indignant eyes. "Don't put it that way, Liz," he said anxiously. "I was worried about you." He was also more than a little shocked at his own behavior.

Holly, trying to control her feelings of helplessness, decided the time had come to test Steven's true motives. She put her hands on his chest, feeling the warmth and strength of his body flow into hers. Snatches of her brother's conversation filtered through her febrile mind. Gradually her anger ebbed, to be replaced by intense feminine curiosity.

She smiled, a fey little female smile, leading Steven to wonder where she *had* taken lessons. She pressed closer, until her breasts brushed against his chest. "Go ahead," she said all of a sudden, surprising him.

Distracted by the heat of her contact, he cleared his throat. "Go ahead . . . what?"

"Go ahead and kiss me," she answered matter-of-factly.

He raised his brow. "Now?" Trusting honey eyes mesmerized him. Why hadn't he noticed those eyes before tonight? *Really* noticed them, he wondered.

"What better time?" she murmured, standing on tiptoe to put her hands around his neck. "It was your idea."

Why hadn't he noticed how husky her voice could get? Or the darkening of her eyes when she invited him to kiss her? This was a new Liz. He was surprised, shocked, pleased. The touch of her fingers in his hair worked their magic clear to his feet. Nevertheless, common sense intruded.

"What about Mark? I hate to start a lesson and be interrupted."

"He'll wait," she assured him huskily, driving him a little bit mad with wanting. She kissed the side of his mouth. "Just think, you're making me better able to please a man. I can't thank you enough for this display of friendship. Not many men are so noble."

He didn't feel noble at all; he felt hot with a sexual awareness. He wanted to rip off her pink dress and throw her on the bed and take her. He wanted to feel her soft skin come alive beneath his hands. He wanted to hear her throaty voice moan that she wanted him. He wanted to kiss her until she cried out. He wanted to turn the bed into a cradle of love. And when he had had his fill, he wanted his life to get back on an even keel. His whole stupid speech about teaching her more about kissing had popped unbidden out of his mouth. He felt her kiss the other side of his mouth. Trying to find an excuse for his passion, he decided it probably had something to do with the damned dress and the sassy way she looked in heels. His eyes dropped downward to the creamy mounds lifting her dress. Since when did she show so much décolletage?

"You're sure?" he asked. He couldn't believe he'd actually said that. What in the world was happening to him? He groaned as she teasingly pressed herself closer.

She threaded her fingers in his hair, loving the luxuriant richness. "Yes, very," she confirmed cheerfully. She kissed the side of his neck, taking little love bites as she did. She chuckled inwardly. Louise would be proud of her unknown pupil.

Her words came out on a breathless whisper. "I couldn't have advertised for a better teacher, now, could I?" She cupped his face between her hands and rained tiny kisses along his jaw. Then she stepped back, lowering her lashes demurely. "And you are so conveniently located—neither one of us has to travel far."

Shocked, he stared down at her for an endless moment. Whatever game she was playing, it took two. His arms wrapped tightly around her. One hand moved to cup her head; the other slipped to her breast, boldly kneading the soft mound.

Holly gasped. She had only a second to consider the possibility of her plan backfiring. Then it became too late to consider anything. She felt his breath mingle with hers as he bent his head, his mouth finding hers in a branding kiss. If she had started out by teasing him, she was soon caught up in her own design. His kisses became sweet torture, sweet madness, demanding more.

His hand slid to her nape, rubbing the soft skin with his thumb. Louise's imaginary advice slipped out of her mind. Everything emptied out of Holly's mind, except Steven and his effect on her warring senses.

She had forgotten to consult her body when she'd conjured up her little plan. Now it reacted as a starved person would to food—barely aware of her thighs moving closer to his, barely aware of her lips opening for his quest, barely aware of her tongue following his lead. She quite simply threw everything she had into the kiss . . . and then some.

She explored his mouth with the same hungry thoroughness he did hers. The heat of his body set off rampaging fires; she drew closer to its heat. In case this was going to be their last kiss, she wanted to store up all the memories she could for the future.

He drew a harsh breath and pushed her away. "I've changed my mind," he said brusquely. "The timing's all wrong."

It took every bit of her reserve, but she forced herself not to let him know that if she weren't leaning against the wall, she'd be on the floor.

Steven's body told her what Steven's lips refused to utter—he *did* want her. If he were ever going to come to grips with his feelings for her, now was the time. All he needed was a dose of the same emotion she'd been grappling with since she'd met him.

Jealousy!

She sighed, nodding her head in pretended agreement. "How many lessons do you think I'll need before I'm launched—so to speak? So that I'd be more attractive to other men, the kind you'd approve of," she asked solemnly.

None, he silently fumed. His system had been jolted by a thunderbolt—in the body of one small package of dynamite. The last time he'd kissed her, she had knocked his socks off. This time, his reaction to her made him yearn for the ice floes of Alaska. He gritted his teeth, willing his sexual urges to stop tormenting him. Where was the comfortable Liz? His friend, who listened to his problems?

The one who wasn't any threat to his single lifestyle.

"How many?" she prompted, happily watching a muscle flex in his jaw.

"Why do you ask?"

She held up her hand to examine a freshly polished pink nail. Puckering her lips in a tiny o, she blew gently on the nail. She acted as if she had all the time in the world to consider her answer. Finally, she drew a deep breath and raised her eyes, letting him see a shade of pity in their brown depths.

"No offense, Steven," she said. "I appreciate what you're trying to do for me and all, but I don't think you're the man to do it." She smiled at him from beneath a curtain of lashes, looking utterly guileless.

"Because," she continued, "I think, if I'm going to learn, I should be taught by a master."

Holly let the implication of her words sink in, timing her next sentence to elevate the shock value. She put her hands on his chest, patting him gently as one would a child.

"You're right, of course," she added sweetly. "I do need lessons. But at my age, I don't have much time to waste. Everything is so much different out here, the pace and all. Naturally . . . I want to learn how to please a man." She patted his cheek, letting a finger trail its side.

"Naturally . . . I want a man to please me too," she said seriously. "Making love should be a cooperative effort, don't you agree? One of the studies I participated in had to do with the male androgen. This little display of your technique . . ." She lifted her shoulders, intimating gentle reproval. "Perhaps you're . . ." She paused portentously, long enough to check on Steven's reaction.

Steven felt as if he'd just been punched out by a butterfly. If he had heard correctly—and he knew damn well he had—Liz had just called to question his manhood, and had also confessed her virginity.

The bed loomed behind him with added meaning.

All his life he had relied on instinct where people were concerned. He had judged character on eye contact, honesty, and a firm handshake. There was something else he was a good judge of—women. Liz did not need lessons. That kiss had affected him. If it had affected him, it had affected her too.

"Fix your lipstick," he said angrily. "It's smudged. I'm going out to the living room before Mark starts wondering what we've been doing in here."

She smiled, with the confidence of a woman who'd soared free for the first time in her life. "No, he won't. It's written all over your lips."

He grabbed the tissue she held and stomped out of the room.

Holly dropped into a chair by the dressing table to repair her lipstick. She was still shaking. Where had she gotten up the nerve to go through with such a ridiculous act? What she had said to him about his kissing ability was the biggest lie she'd ever told in her life. If her insides were any judge of ability, Steven scored somewhere in the stratosphere. Her heaving breasts were evidence of the lie; so were the butterflies in her stomach.

But, once and for all, she wanted Steven to face some facts. She couldn't be so much in love with him without him feeling anything for her. A little soul-searching on his part wouldn't hurt.

Holly began her own soul-searching, and within moments her sense of euphoria was replaced by a full-fledged letdown. True, Steven had come on to her like a jealous lover, but he had never once asked her out for a bona fide date!

So what did this all mean? she asked herself miserably. *It meant,* her conscience explained, *that Steven came simply to tell you about Santos. He saw you all dressed up for once, and he was surprised. That's all it meant.*

You, she told her mirror image, *did all the rest by yourself. You threw yourself at him shamelessly. The man never did a thing to you under false pretenses. His offer to teach you how to kiss was just macho preening.*

But why her though? What did he want from her life? True, she had a few truths to tell him, but he had some truths he needed to face too. Friend or lover, it was high time he stopped taking her for granted!

She touched her flushed face with the back of her shaking hand. It was several moments before her hand was steady enough to control the lip liner to outline her lips. When she was through applying the pink-toned lipstick, she dabbed her swollen lips with gloss.

She was embarrassed by her foolhardy actions, and she reaffirmed her original plan. As long as

Mark had already accepted Steven's invitation, she'd live through the evening, somehow. But as soon as Mark left town, she'd tell Steven everything.

Then, she'd wash her hands of the whole affair. She wasn't cut out for subterfuge—her nerves couldn't take the strain. She had tried, really tried to do the right thing, but Mark was right. Steven was a man. He could fight his own battles. She was on the firing range with bullets coming from both sides! And if there was one thing she'd learned since working for Digger, it was that commitments are defined differently in Tinseltown!

Nine

Holly insisted that Mark sit in the front seat with Steven. "It's only right, Steven. After all, Mark's the tourist." As Steven opened the rear door for her, he leaned over so only she could hear. "Coward," he chuckled. Then he patted her rear end.

The man was a mind reader!

The truth was, she needed time to think about how she would present the facts to him. She still felt shaken from their encounter; it was all she could do to control a wild desire to tell him to turn the car around so they could go back to the bedroom and finish what they had started.

"What do you think, Liz?"

"What do I think about what?" she asked, shaken out of her reverie.

"Which CD would you rather hear? 'Bridge Over Troubled Waters,' or 'Anything For Love'?"

She refrained from asking if he had "The Truth Shall Set You Free," by a little-known female trio. "Whatever you want is all right with me."

Steven sent her a heated glance through the rearview mirror. "I'm going to hold you to that."

He furnished a running commentary for Mark's benefit; during lulls in the conversation, he whistled. There was no doubt in her mind he was up to something. From the moment they had left the apartment, when he had placed his hand firmly at the small of her back to guide her into the elevator and then wrapped his big hand over hers as they made their descent to the garage, she knew it without a doubt. She knew him well enough to know that when he whistled, the wheels were turning in his brain. The other shoe was about to fall—it was simply a question of when.

She sat, tense and anxious, in the rear of the Mercedes, listening to Steven ask questions about her as a child. She didn't even feel like interrupting or speaking for herself. She just didn't care. But when Mark described her in saccharine tones as the most dependable, virtuous, thoughtful, caring, honest person a family could hope for, she was surprised he didn't also add: *We'll love her regardless!*

"That's my Lizzy," Steven said when Mark finished.

Mark coughed.

Steven whistled.

Holly groaned. She wouldn't be in this mess if it weren't for Digger, the little twerp. He'd put a double whammy on her. How could she have been so naive? First, he'd set her up as an incognito "investigative reporter," insisting she wear a wig. Then, when she'd kept dragging her feet, not furnishing the information, he'd dreamt up Hortense. And finally, he had accused her of wanting Steven for herself.

That part was true. She did want him—desperately! She tuned in and then tuned out the conversation in the front seat. Under other circumstances, she would have found the repartee between these two very similar men interesting. They seemed to be cut from the same cloth—both bright, both sharing a dry sense of humor, both enjoying each other's company.

Maybe she was becoming paranoid, but it seemed to her that the nicer Steven acted, the more she wondered how long he planned to dangle the rope before he yanked it. She should have remembered the phrase: Don't get mad, get even!

She suddenly remembered that Hortense was supposed to show up Monday! She did some quick calculations; assuming Steven was busy tomorrow, she'd have to wait until Monday night to talk with him. Tonight was no good—she needed her wits about her. By the time they'd get home, she'd be too wiped-out. It was bad enough to confess she was a blonde using a partially different name; how in the world was she going to explain Hortense? Maybe she'd make it easy on herself and let Hortense write Steven another one of her notes:

Dear Mr. Chadwick,
    I can't continue working for you. I'm going

to graduate school. I'll miss you, especially since you started hanging up your clothes!

Hortense

With such a bleak future, was it any wonder her head ached!

Steven pulled the car to a stop in front of La Mama's. The liveried valet hurried over to assist Holly from the car but Steven smoothly moved him to the side, helping her himself. He firmly tucked her hand in his as they made their way toward the canopied door.

The maître d' greeted Steven warmly and led them to the best available table in the dimly lit nightclub. Steven looked around the room and said, "You get your wish, Mark; there's Trish Cole, the movie star."

Mark followed Steven's gaze and let out a low wolf whistle. Even without bright lights, it was easy to see the talented actress was gorgeous. The moment she spied Steven, she came over to give him a big kiss.

Steven grinned. "Can you join us?"

Trish Cole's stunning green eyes locked with Steven's. Then her gaze slid over to Mark, liking what she saw. "Yes; my friends want to go on to Reanne's, but I'd much rather stay here and dance. The music is more romantic."

Holly felt the beginning of a storm raging inside her. Trish fit the bill of the mystery blonde! Trish's long tresses matched the hairs she'd plucked from Steven's pillow. While Holly boiled over the sexy blonde's obvious ease with Steven, the singer on the small raised stage—who looked as if she had been poured into her red sequined dress—was begging everyone in throaty tones to "Hold me tight."

Steven pushed back his chair and held out his hand. He led Holly onto the small dance floor, where he held her, tight and close and intimate. He was an expert dancer with a natural grace and style. They swayed to the music; he shifted her closer. With the lightest of touches, his fingers rode up to the side of her breast. With the slightest pressure, he kissed her lips. He was using every unfair tactic in the book.

This game he was playing was a close encounter of the worst kind—shockingly intimate, pushing her beyond reason . . . making her want him. She wanted him to know her as intimately as a man could know a woman.

And she wanted to know him and explore his body the same way.

"Loosen up, sweet. I thought you said you loved to dance?"

Holly couldn't loosen up. She was consumed by jealousy and other rioting emotions. "Do women usually come here unescorted?" she asked, averting her gaze.

He chucked her under the chin; it was enough to increase her heartbeat. "I take it you're referring to Trish. I do believe you're jealous—we're making progress."

"I'm not jealous." She felt herself turn crimson, but she had to know. "Have you two ever been an item?"

He grinned a little, then took a nibble from the side of her mouth. "You *are* jealous!"

Holly humphed. His uncanny perception at reading her mind was too much! Steven laughed and held her tighter. When she tried to wiggle away, he bent down and whispered. "Don't do that. It's sure to awaken my androgens!"

"Steven—believe me, I'm sorry I ever brought that up!"

"There you go again," he teased, "talking dirty."

"What am I going to do with you?" She laughed in spite of herself.

"You've got that wrong. It's what *we* are going to do *together*." His voice was low and seductive and certain.

"Can we sit this one out?" she pleaded. "I'm going to need my energy for tomorrow."

His eyes were full of promise. "Wrong," he said swiftly, "you're going to need your energy for later." He held her close, keeping her hips near his, letting her know exactly what he meant. "Besides, I like holding you. It's all part of the foreplay to making love. You know that's where this is leading, don't you?"

"Steven," she whispered, "we're barely moving now."

"*Shhhh*," he told her, nuzzling her neck. "Listen to the words." He hummed them in her ear. " 'Hold me tight. Wrap your arms around me . . . hold me through the night.' That's what I'm going to do to you. You have nothing to be afraid of—I'll make it beautiful for you. The first time should always be memorable."

Holly was thankful the other couples on the small dance floor were occupied in their own little worlds. Steven had correctly guessed she was a virgin; she could only hope he attributed her nervousness to that. Nothing was going the way it was supposed to.

Steven seemed to read her thoughts. "Relax, honey. We'll talk later. Let's enjoy this while we can."

She worked hard to put a clamp on her emotions, to try to steer clear of wishful thinking. Her feelings terrified her. They were new and powerful and excitingly primitive.

In a way, she couldn't wait until the evening was over. And in another way, she wanted it to last forever. She was in the eye of a hurricane, the calm before the storm. She wanted memories.

She closed her eyes, drifting along on the sheer, intoxicating pleasure of being in his arms. She felt his fingers intimately riding her spine, fitting her closer to him. She heard his heartbeat thrumming beneath her ear where her cheek rested on his chest. She breathed in the woodsy aroma of his aftershave lotion.

And she stored her memories.

When the song ended, they looked deeply into one another's eyes. It was as if each were coming to a momentous decision concerning their fates.

Suddenly, there was a flurry of activity in the entryway, the kind of activity that usually accompanied a major star. Holly glanced behind Steven.

Digger! She felt the color drain from her face.

Her nerves tailspinned. Digger was here! Outfitted in a white suit with a red silk shirt and a red carnation in his lapel, he had just made his entrance into the room with a famous actress on his arm!

Holly cursed herself for her stupidity. Why hadn't she remembered that Digger made the rounds of the clubs each night?

Steven interrupted her wild thoughts. "Honey, do you want to go back to the table for a drink?"

Drink! Right now she needed ten. Her eyes darted over to the people gathering around the star. No way was she going to go back to their table. It was too close to where Digger was standing. "No. Let's dance some more."

"My pleasure. What's that noise?" He started to turn, but Holly grabbed his arms.

"Nothing, come on. This is my favorite song."

"Mine too," he said. Holly heard the words: "I've got you under my skin, I've got you deep in the heart of me."

She had no time to blush—Digger was closing in on them. Digger, with the uncanny ability of a homing pigeon about to deliver a secret, coded message, found Holly's eyes and delivered his.

Holly knew he expected a full report on Monday, unless he planned on demanding one in the next few minutes!

She couldn't let Steven see Digger. Between Digger's accusing her of feathering her own nest and Steven's accusing her of having an aging lover, Holly saw the firing squad poised at the ready.

She reacted—by throwing her arms around his

neck. "Steven," she confessed, "I can't stand this." She would beg his forgiveness. She wouldn't wait until the weekend was over. Never, ever in her whole life would she even try to do a good deed again unless all parties knew what she was doing. She swore this on Robin Hood's grave.

Steven obligingly wrapped his arms around her waist.

"I can't either, honey. Besides, it's getting too damn noisy in here. What do you think we should do about it? Would Mark mind if we left him here with Trish?"

Left him with Trish? Holly was borderline hysterical. Steven was assuming that she wanted to leave because she had the hots for him! Which she did—but not while Digger was breathing down her neck.

Then she saw Digger lift his arm to wave. He made a thumbs-up sign and, to top it off, he blew her a kiss!

"Steven, I want you to kiss me," she demanded. "Here?"

She saw Digger approaching. "I can't wait until later. I'm ready for my next lesson. Kiss me!" She grabbed Steven's face between her hands. "Now!" she demanded.

Steven reacted quickly. His mouth opened on hers, taking what she readily offered. Around them, people chuckled. Meanwhile, Holly loosened one of her arms. She waved frantically, hoping Mark would see her. He'd have to realize trouble was afoot.

At the last second, Mark caught her frantic signal and waylaid Digger. Like an avenging angel, he placed his arm around Digger's shoulders, greeting the startled columnist like a long-lost buddy.

From the corner of her eye, Holly saw Mark guide Digger toward the bar, out of harm's way. Coming up for air, she let her head rest on Steven's chest. Now all she had to do was maneuver them out of there in one piece.

For once she agreed with Digger—Minneapolis was never like this. She pushed away from Steven, gulping. "Let's go home."

"Liz, stop acting so jumpy. I told you before I'd take care of you. Making love is not something to get over with."

"Can we *please* go home?" she pleaded.

"All right, honey," he soothed, "we're going home."

Steven stopped to speak quietly with Mark, who nodded, then walked over to Holly while Steven paid the bill. "Are you going to be all right?" he asked. She assured him she was, temporarily. But then, it was anybody's guess how Steven would react.

"He's a good man, Holly. He loves you."

She could have told him otherwise, but didn't.

"What did you say to Digger?"

"I explained to him that I was your brother. I told him you've taken me into your confidence, and asked me to assure him you are very close to wrapping up the case." He shook his head for a second, laughing at himself. "I can't believe I used that term. Anyway, I strongly suggested that it would be better not to interfere at such a critical time. Then I told him I couldn't wait to read the book."

Holly scoffed. "That'll be the day! I want you to swear to me, Mark, if I ever try to mind someone else's business again, you'll tie me up and gag me. After tonight, Steven's going to hate me."

"Sis, the man loves you—stop worrying. There isn't going to be any war."

"From your lips to God's ears." She didn't want to be locked in combat with Steven. She wanted to be locked in his arms, making love.

Ten

Steven squeezed Liz's hand, feeling its coolness. He glanced at her; as the car sped through the night, passing street lamps sent a play of light and shadow over her face.

The telltale nervous signs were there—the taut interlacing of her fingers, the gripping of her hands when she thought he was unaware, even her occasional little sighs. He wanted to tell her not to be afraid, that what was going to happen between them was right and good. He thought of the first time they'd met, how he had held her on his lap, soothing away her fears. Tonight he would hold her in his arms, changing her fears to passion. He felt the tug of his own passion, sharp and welcome. It was all part of it . . . all part of the prelude.

He pressed down on the gas pedal, then steered

the conversation to a light topic, as much for her as for himself. He reached over to pat her hand. "Who's your favorite singer?"

Holly jolted. The little tremor in her stomach came from her active imagination; the question had interrupted her flow of thoughts. "What?" She caught herself lacing her fingers together, and stopped.

"Your favorite singer?" The tape played Reba McEntire's "Last To Know."

How does he do it? she wondered. How did he always manage to play music precisely about their relationship? "I have a crush on Placido Domingo," she admitted.

Steven raised his eyebrows. "It's a good thing he's a continent away, then." He informed her that his favorite opera was Puccini's Madame Butterfly.

"I pegged you for a cowboy-music man." She welcomed the easy banter, glad for the diversion. She turned her head and met his gaze, blurting out suddenly, "I have a secret yen to visit Elvis Presley's home, Graceland."

He promised himself to take her there. "Domingo and Presley," he mused. "That's quite a contrast."

Indulging herself, she reacted by challenging, "So's opera and 'Home On The Range.' "

He chuckled. "We all have our little secrets, don't we?"

Holly caught herself lacing her fingers again.

Steven parked the car in the garage. He came around to her side, helping her out. As they walked hand in hand up the flight of stairs, Holly's heightened senses measured sounds. The laughter of a group of young people in a passing car. The blast of a car horn. The shrill siren of a police car racing through the night streets. The rhythmic footfall of her heels on the cool, Italian marble floor in the sumptuous lobby. The whisper of silk against her skin as they made their way to the bank of elevators.

She was more aware of Steven than ever, more conscious of how each of them wanted the evening to end. So, like a miser, she began to tally and tuck away her memories for safekeeping: for tomorrow, when she would leave Mason's apartment; for next week, when she would bid goodbye to California; for all the months and years to come when she'd be without Steven—when she'd be empty.

She had come full circle—it had all begun in this lobby when she'd stood by his side, waiting for an elevator to whisk her to her fate.

And now she was waiting for an elevator again. As then, she was acutely aware of the tall, handsome man by her side, but now she knew more about him. There was more to cherish; certainly more to lose. She would miss his breezy laugh, his boyish good humor—even his bossy manner. She would miss his familiar rap on the door; miss the way his eyes lit up as if he were delighted to see her waiting for him.

Digger had correctly chosen him as a prize person for some lucky woman to marry. Steven's wife would know a loving relationship. Since he was concerned primarily with wealth, Digger's reasons for wanting to write about Steven fell far short of the mark. They failed to capture the essence of the man. Steven was the most interesting, intelligent, caring person she'd ever met. And she would miss him every day of her life.

Searching for an opening line, she tried to envision the coming scene.

Steven, I have the most amazing story to tell you. . . .

Rubbish! her conscience taunted. *You've always prided yourself on honesty. You could have quit anytime!* But if I had, her mind countered, *I wouldn't have been able to help Steven.*

Half-truths! the voice of her conscience ruthlessly challenged. *We both know part of the reason you stayed on was because you couldn't bear to be away from him.*

No more half-truths, she promised. No more bargains with her conscience. She'd start at the beginning, she'd find the middle, and hurry to the end. After that, she'd take her chances. If the romantic side of her wished for a happy ending, the realistic side of her knew her chances for happiness after Steven learned the truth were slim. She deliberately forced herself to remember the good times.

Steven's gaze skimmed over Liz's trim figure and back up to her face. Falling in love was a joyful shock, he mused. He hadn't expected it to creep up on him. He was a mature man with a certain sense of cynicism, and he'd arrived at an age where he thought it wouldn't happen. But it had, with the force of a sledgehammer, surprising the hell out of him.

He studied her face, marveling again at her classic bone structure, her fine skin coloring—she radiated vitality. Familiar stirrings tugged his senses. Then, as if she knew he was thinking about her, she glanced up at him and blushed.

In that instant, he envisioned their lives inextricably intertwined, celebrating the pleasures and yes, even the sadness. They would weather it all, because they'd have each other.

So this is what love is, he realized—fires dancing around his heart. He was glad that love had come first in the guise of friendship. They were lucky; too many couples were like meteors hurtling through the sky, only to splinter in a shower of broken dreams.

He would ask her to marry him. His lips moved in a warm smile. He applied a slight pressure to Liz's fingers, pulling her attention back to him again. "Do you remember the first time?"

She returned his smile, her honey-chestnut eyes correctly surmising his meaning. "You hated me," she stated.

He lifted a negative brow as his palm caressed her face. How could he hate the person more dear to him than anyone in the world? He touched her lips with his, shushing her. "I didn't hate you," he protested, not leaving her lips until he had claimed them a second time.

She twinkled. "You did—you know it. You waved your handkerchief at me and insisted I take it. I think you were afraid I'd give you pneumonia.

And then I crashed into you." She giggled. "I thought you were going to strangle me."

He tilted back his head and roared. He loved the feisty way she challenged him. "You're right," he admitted, toying with the idea of kissing the smug grin off her face.

"Of course I am," she said.

He slipped his arm around her shoulder, drawing her closer. "But then you needed my help, and everything changed. Do you remember deciding to make out your will?"

She bumped her hip against him. "Don't you dare make fun of me!"

His eyes danced. "I couldn't believe you wanted to write a letter to a dog."

She poked his ribs, her eyes mirroring his teasing mood. "Not just any dog, smartie—Oscar."

He locked his arms on either side of her, making her his nonprotesting prisoner. "You're lucky I didn't strangle you when you came up with the brilliant idea of standing on my back. Didn't anyone ever tell you that high heels in the small of the back feel like a sword being rammed into you?"

She rested her hands on his arms, reaching up on her tiptoes to plant a kiss at the base of his neck. "Well, you got even." Her soft laughter was infectious, fueling his.

He drew her closer. He ran his hands down her sides, loving it when her eyes suddenly darkened. "I was only saving your life with the guggle muggle. I have it,"—he leaned his forehead against hers—"on the best authority,"—he nibbled the corner of her mouth—"that the guggle muggle is responsible for all of this. I never would have had a reason to check on you so often if you hadn't been on the brink of pneumonia. I say, three cheers for the guggle muggle!"

She made an impish face. "And I say, phooey!"

He reached for her again, but she drew back from him on a breathless laugh, averting her face. "Steven," she scolded, "suppose the elevator comes and the door opens and there are people in it?"

He matched her seriousness with a mocking imitation. "I'll tell them I've been hired as your teacher to show you the finer points of kissing."

She rolled her eyes. "You're never going to let me forget that, are you?"

He grinned. "Nope. Let's just say I've planned a full course of study. If I ever let you graduate, then—and only then—will I consider accepting your apology."

She touched his face with her finger. "How did you get the scar near your lip?"

He flashed her a very appealing grin. "In a fight."

The elevator door slid open; he automatically tucked her hand in his.

"We're going to my place."

The quiet, sure way Steven stated his intentions brought the real purpose of the evening back into sharp focus for Holly.

She remained silent as he ushered her into his apartment. She glanced around at the clean living room. Hortense had certainly made a neater man out of Steven. That, she thought, as she trailed after him into the game room, was an accomplishment. Steven had been paying attention to Hortense's notes.

He stepped behind the gleaming mahogany bar. "Look around while I fix us a drink," he said, removing two Waterford glasses from a shelf. "There are a lot of interesting things here."

She did, mostly because she noticed two items were missing. What had Steven done with the small painting of the mystery blonde? And where on earth was the merry-go-round horse?

Steven came to her side. "We'll take these into the living room—it's more comfortable. Unless you'd prefer a guided tour?"

Holly took a deep breath, cutting off until later the admission that she knew every inch of the apartment. "No tour. The living room is fine for now." She sat down in a wing chair and lifted an unsteady hand to sip her drink. "We have to talk. I want you to sit over there and listen to what I have to say. Please," she begged. "This is very hard for me."

He looked over at her, noting how genuinely upset she was. His smile vanished, and he came over to her and bent down. He took the glass from her hand and put it on the Queen Anne table near the chair.

"Sweetheart, maybe if I tell you how I feel about you, it will make this easier. Liz, I love you."

She gasped and started to speak. He kissed her quickly, stilling her. He had never said those words to another woman, and he wasn't going to let anything stop him now.

"It's true. It's been happening right from the start, only I was too blind to see it."

He rubbed his thumbs over her palms. "Sweetheart, we don't have to discuss this, you know. I realize you've waited a long time. Frankly, I'm glad you did, but I think it's made you more apprehensive than you need to be. Sex doesn't have to be talked to death. Between two people who love each other—" He stopped, interrupting himself with a look of concern. "You *do* love me, don't you?"

Her eyes were luminous. "Oh, yes," she said softly.

He relaxed. "Then, darling, nothing else matters."

"Oh," she moaned, "don't say that. Not yet."

Steven drew her out of the chair. He needed to let her know how he felt. He fit her body to his; this time he wasn't patient. He let his aroused body tell her how much he needed her. He ground her hips to him as his mouth ignored anything but the fever burning in him.

She twisted her head, breaking the kiss. "Steven," she pleaded, "give me a few minutes. I won't be long."

She went into the bathroom, stood before the mirror, and removed a small hairbrush from her purse. She yanked off the hated wig and dumped it into the wastepaper basket. She ran her fingers through her hair, reveling in the freedom of being herself. Then she brushed her hair until it was a mass of shining gold.

For years she had wondered how she'd feel when the time came to trust her love and her body to a special man. When she emerged from this room, she'd be taking the most serious gamble of her life. If she couldn't make Steven understand, she'd never know that special closeness with him. With a final check in the mirror, she took a deep breath and left the room.

Steven wasn't in the living room; somehow, it didn't surprise her. She followed the thin beam of light leading to the master suite, pausing in the doorway. How often had she dreamed of coming to him in this room?

The skylight was open. A soft breeze flowed into the room, causing a faint rustle of sound. She looked up. A circlet of stars surrounded the full moon. Her glance slid away. The coverlet on the king-size bed was turned down; their drinks were on the night table near the bed.

He was standing near the window. She took a moment to appreciate the sheer male beauty of him, letting her eyes roam over his magnificent body. His naked back was to her. There was an air of quiet strength about him. Softly, slowly, she reached out to him.

He knew she was there. He knew her by her scent, by her special magic—the magic that from now on would only be for him. He purposely remained with his back to her. He wanted to give her time, to let her get used to the idea of seeing him waiting for her.

"Steven,"—he heard the quiver in her voice—
"turn around."

He did. He started to go to her, then froze. The
woman standing in the doorway was a different
Liz. This golden goddess was how he'd dreamed
Liz's coloring was meant to be. For a split second,
reality fled. He just stared at her in astonishment.
She was heartbreakingly beautiful—and obviously
frightened.

It was her fear that took the edge off his shock.
It was her fear that pulled his feet forward, even
before the questions spilling over in his brain
rolled to the tip of his tongue. "Liz?"

She moved toward him with fluid grace. "I . . . I
didn't know how else to tell you." He repeated her
name. "It's me," she soothed. "I'm not a mirage.
This is what I've been trying to tell you."

He let his hands touch the strands of gold,
marveling at its glorious shade. "I don't understand. Why did you hide this behind a wig?"

"I've been trying to explain. . . ."

He cupped her hair in his hands. "This is what
you've been trying to tell me? That day in the
park?"

"Yes," she said, welcoming the loving gesture.

He buried his face in her hair. "The time I fell
asleep on the couch?"

"Yes." She clung to him in relief. She knew he
needed to touch her, to acquaint himself with the
way she really looked. She would wait a moment
longer before surprising him again.

He chuckled. "And I thought you were nervous
because you're a virgin."

She kissed him softly on the lips. The words came out on a sigh. "I am." She trembled.

He touched her hair again. "Darling, you're more beautiful than ever."

He let his eyes roam over her. He lifted her shining mass of hair again, letting it shower through his fingers. His hands ran gently over her back, exciting her even as she struggled to stop him.

"Steven, there's more. I just wanted you to see the real me when I tell you the rest."

"I can't get over it." He quickly skimmed his fingers over her shapely form.

"What are you doing?"

"Making sure you're not a boy in drag—are you?"

She giggled then, breaking some of the tension. "No, I can guarantee I'm not a boy." For the first time, she allowed herself to hope.

He let out a comic sigh of relief. He took her hand and led her to the bed. Kicking off his shoes, he drew her down beside him. "If there are any more surprises, I'd better be lying down."

She snuggled close to him. "My name is not Elizabeth Mason." She heard him suck in his breath, but he said nothing. "Part of it is. My real name is Holly Elizabeth Anderson."

"What? I thought perhaps you and Mark had different fathers." Steven looked her full in the eye. He shook his head, as if he didn't believe what he was hearing. She tenderly let her fingers touch his cheek.

"I was working on a case. I used Tom Mason's apartment while he's in Europe."

Steven scowled. He shifted to his side, propping himself up on an elbow for support. "You're going too fast for me. A case? What kind of case? Are you some kind of detective?"

She shook her head. She ran her hand up his arm, over his shoulder, to cup his face.

"A spy?" There was real concern mingled with confusion in his eyes.

"Do you remember the man you called the old geek?"

"Sure I do," he scoffed. "He *is* an old geek."

"He's more than that. He's my boss. He's the reason I moved to California in the first place. He's also the person who put me in Mason's apartment. You do remember I told you my life was boring and I wanted some excitement? Well, I got more than I bargained for."

She began to talk. She told him she was truly a researcher, but that she worked for Digger Danville. "Have you heard of him?"

"*Ummmm.*" Steven rolled closer; their bodies touched. His hand trailed down her hip to her thigh. "Everybody's heard of Digger," he said, kissing her shoulder. "Louise says he's a creep with power. He uses his column as a personal weapon."

Holly drew a deep breath. "He assigned me to you, telling me you were my very own bachelor."

His fingers halted their journey. He waited.

"He's also the reason I've been wearing the wig," she explained cautiously. "If Liz was unsuccessful in getting an interview to find out about your private life, I was supposed to come back to you as Holly. Digger thought having me play a dual role would be cheaper."

Impatience and disappointment shimmered. "What interview? Why is he interested in me? I'm no actor."

She expelled a deep breath, dreading her next words. "Digger wants information about your private life for his book."

Steven sat up with a jolt. He stared at her. "His book!" he shouted angrily. "What book?"

She winced. The words spilled out in a rush. "The one he's writing on the lifestyles of rich, eligible bachelors. It's a how-to guide for women, and you were at the top of the list."

Steven uttered a string of oaths, his eyes widening in outrage. "And you agreed to this?"

She tossed her head, sending a spray of gold around her shoulders. "I *didn't* agree to it. I told Digger I'd ask you for an interview."

Steven interrupted her. "But you've never asked to interview me."

She nodded. "After we met, the way we met . . . things got all mixed-up. We became friends. Forgive me, Steven; I didn't want to spy on you, but I didn't want Digger to assign someone else to the story. I just pretended to be gathering information."

He seethed. "I'm going to kill that bastard. Why didn't you tell me the truth?"

She couldn't hide her disappointment; the bitterness in his eyes shook her. She couldn't subject herself to seeing the love die in his eyes. She sat up, swinging her legs over the side of the bed. She sighed heavily. It was over. "As I said, I tried. Now you have the essentials you need. I'd better go."

His hand gripped her upper arm. She tried to pull away, but his grip was iron. "You're not going anywhere," he ordered. "Do you think it's easy for me to learn all this? Hell, your name isn't even Liz."

Her chin thrust upward. "Do you imagine it's been easy for me? I've been playing two ends against the middle. On the one hand, I've been stalling Digger; on the other, I've been waiting for the right moment to tell you. Something always interfered. Then, during the weeks you were so worried about business, I didn't have the heart to tell you." Her shoulders sagged. "What I did made perfect sense to me at the time."

He tucked his finger beneath her chin. His look was hard and intense. "You did all this to keep Digger from intruding on my privacy?"

Her mouth trembled. "I thought I did. In the beginning, I did it because I couldn't be part of his snooping, and I honestly wanted to interview you. Digger scoffed at me; he made fun of my principles every chance he got. He said this is how things are done out here. Anyway, later, my reasons changed."

"Go on," Steven probed. His eyes demanded everything.

She bit her lip. She could hear her heartbeat increase. There was the briefest of silences before she quietly added, "You see, I fell in love with you almost from the first moment I saw you. I used the excuse of trying to protect you to cover up the fact that I couldn't bear the thought of not being with you. You were the only reason I didn't quit working for Digger long ago. You also have the right to know that he's accused me of trying to feather my own nest." Drained, she waited for Steven's response. Her eyes filled with tears.

Steven said nothing for a moment. He closed his eyes. He saw the woman who had sought his hand for reassurance each time they rode the elevator. Then he pictured her in the role of fearless defender, slayer of dragons. If she had wanted to feather her own nest, they'd have been in bed long ago; Digger was totally wrong on that score. He tried to picture life without her, and he couldn't—she was too much a part of him. He glanced up to find her looking at him. His eyes softened, letting the essence of her goodness replace everything else.

"You're not angry with me?" Holly asked anxiously.

He laid his hand on her cheek. "For trying to slay the dragons? For keeping Digger from writing about my private life? No, I'm not angry, not really. In a crazy way, I'm honored you would do this for me." His hands spanned her tiny waistline. "Although it's a little strange having someone half my size ride shotgun for me. I still want to get a good swing at Digger." He enfolded her in his arms. "Come over here where you belong."

She clung to him as relief washed over her.

"Darling," she said, nibbling his neck, "if you want to punch him, will you please do it later? Unless you have a serious need to discuss this further, would you please kiss me now?"

He pulled her on top of him until she was stretched over his body like a cat. A cloud of blond hair caped their faces. "It's going to take practice calling you Holly. If I do, will you promise me to consider a different full-time occupation? One which will take up most of your days and all of your nights? Will you marry me?"

Holly's lips curved in a radiant smile. Her eyes sparkled with joy.

"Is that a yes?"

She lowered her lips for his kiss. "A definite yes. You have no idea how I've dreamed about this moment."

"No more than I," he said huskily. He slowly unzipped her dress, kissing her satiny shoulder. "Do you like this?" he murmured as his lips explored all of her. With only his lips on her skin he made her shake, made her tremble—made the tiny coil of tension build and build.

Desire for him swelled up. "Steven . . ."

"Close your eyes," he instructed. "Feel how your body responds to me. It's going to be better than your wildest dreams. I promise . . . just trust me."

With his hands and his lips, he cherished her. He was starving for her. He kissed her eyes and her throat, whispering how beautiful she was. His tongue plunged into her mouth, letting it mate with hers in a love dance. She moved instinctively, reaching for him. She gasped when he moved the hem of her teddy aside, discovering her honeyed warmth; he played her senses until her body was liquid. His lips moved to her breast, suckling first one nipple and then the other through the lace teddy. His breath seared her skin, making it impossible for her to think. She only wanted to feel, to taste, to give in to the pounding of her heart and the impossible coil building in the center of her being.

His lips skimmed over her body, forming the background music to the central beat he orchestrated between her thighs. A sound that was almost a plea for release escaped her lips . . . and then it happened. She arched, shuddering in his arms until the storm receded.

Moonlight filtered down onto the bed. Steven was watching her face, his eyes dark with desire. Blushing from embarrassment, she turned her head into his shoulder.

"Don't ever be embarrassed in front of me, darling. What just happened to you was right and natural. I made that happen for you; it gave me intense pleasure for it to happen for you."

"But . . ." She *was* embarrassed. She couldn't help it. "What about you? What about? . . ."

He kissed the top of her head. "There's plenty of time. We have all night." He heard her sigh of pleasure. "I can't believe we're here together, in love and planning to marry. Wait until my family meets you, and your brother. My mother will love you, and my sister Ginger will probably have a crush on Mark. I'm sorry I wasn't here when she stayed over—I'd have introduced the two of you. You and she have a lot in common; in fact, she's a blonde too."

Holly quickly scooted out from under Steven's shoulder. "When was she here?"

"You remember the weekend I was gone? She and a friend slept over. In fact, that ditzy kid sister of mine left some of her clothes here. Wait a minute," he leaned over, opening the drawer in the night table. "Here's a painting of her. I've been meaning to send it to my mother."

Holly was giddy with happiness. Steven had cleared up the mystery of the blonde! To Steven's delight, Holly began to rain kisses all over his chest, his eyes, his cheeks, and his mouth.

"Steven, I absolutely love you!"

His leg moved over her, and he felt the pain of his arousal. His eyes darkened with passion. "Good, because I absolutely love you too." He practiced saying her name. "Holly, I don't know whether you've noticed it or not, but . . ."

She glanced down, blushing again. She read the desire in his eyes, answering it with her own. Hot and hard, he came back to her, letting her know how she excited him. "No clothes now—I want to see you naked. I want to feel all of you." He began to stroke her, slipping the teddy from her shoulders as he did. He shifted for a moment, shrugging out of his trousers and his briefs.

He was magnificent! She opened her arms to welcome him; naked flesh met naked flesh. Hands and lips exchanged pleasure points as he taught her the rich, full meaning of love between a man and a woman. He led her to feelings she'd never dreamed possible.

"Do you like this?" he whispered.

"Oh, yes," she answered shyly.

He kissed her, leaving her gasping at the intimacy. "And there?"

"Ahh, yes," she murmured.

He stroked the silken skin between her thighs. "And here?"

"Oh, yes . . . yes, yes."

He watched her, wanting her with such a savagery it surprised him. She was his drug, he couldn't get enough of her. Her body tasted like jasmine and gold. He held back, straining.

"Don't be afraid," he murmured. "Don't be afraid to touch me too."

Shyly, her hands found him. He sucked in his breath from the innocent way she inflamed him. The breeze from the skylight touched his back, but it didn't cool his burning flesh. Her face was damp and flushed, her eyes closed tight. He moved his knee between her legs, and her eyes fluttered open, her body tensed.

"No—don't be afraid. I told you I'd make it good for you. Trust me."

The plea in his voice touched her heart. He was telling her he'd be with her. He was asking for her love, her trust. She smiled, and moved her thighs to accommodate him.

He told her again that he loved her, until he felt her relax. He kissed her deeply, moving gently inside her, letting her adjust to his fullness. With his body he stoked the flames, over and over, until they burned out of control.

A cry escaped her lips. Her nails dug into his back as she strived toward the unknown, knowing only that she'd die if she didn't reach it. His mouth found one naked breast, then another, sending her on up another dizzying crest toward the summit.

He felt her muscles tighten around him; he knew the miracle would be happening for her soon. He had wanted this for her, wanted her to know how it would always be for them. Even as his own fires ignited out of control, erupting inside him, he rejoiced because it was happening for her too.

Holly lay limp, her muscles relaxed. Breathless, she watched the sky spin above her. The musky smell of passion misted over the bed.

He kissed her forehead. "How do you feel?" His voice was tender.

Her voice was filled with wonder. "Triumphant. As if I know a great secret."

His hand dropped on her thigh, feeling the silken skin.

"Is it always this way?" she asked, curious.

He wanted to hear her say it. "What way?"

She gazed at him through lashes partly lowered. "Wonderful. As if you knew you'd be shattering in a million pieces, and couldn't stand it if you didn't."

He smiled. He had his answer. He tilted her chin, kissing her. "With us, it will always be."

She was quiet for a while, content to play with

the hair on his chest. Then, after a while, she coyly asked, "When do I get my next lesson?"

He slapped her rump, laughing. "Don't get too cocky. You might not be able to walk too easily in the morning."

Her laugh was teasingly low; she felt terrific. "In my studies at the university—" she began slowly.

"Shut up, darling. Or I'll have to prove to you that what you learned about androgens was a lot of crap."

She kissed his chin. "Is that a promise or a threat?"

He pulled the covers up over them, nibbling his way up her delicious body. "Give me a little while. Maybe it'll be both."

He wrapped his arms around her, drawing her to his side. She heard his deep breathing and snuggled closer. Holly sighed and counted her blessings. She thought of this lovely room, where this lovely man had taken her on an age-old journey. And she thought of all the memories to come.

And then, with a start, she realized she'd completely forgotten to tell Steven about Hortense!

Eleven

The sun streamed through the open skylight onto the bed. Steven paused in the doorway, feasting his eyes on the woman he loved. Her hair looked wild, and there was a smile on her face and a flush on her cheeks. Responsible for all three, he felt pretty proud of himself.

"Good morning, Sleeping Beauty. I trust you spent a good night?"

Holly opened an eye and laughed. Steven was quite a sight. He had a huge grin on his face, a bath towel around his waist, Liz's brown wig perched atop his head, and a glass of freshly squeezed orange juice in his hand.

"Wipe that astonished look off your face. I fished this thing out of the garbage."

"Why? I hate that wig." Stretching luxuriously,

she felt glorious, reborn. The world was exciting and safe and filled with love—all because of Steven.

Steven wiggled his brow. Then he leaned over and planted a juicy kiss on Holly's lips. His eyes twinkled. "This wig is going to be saved in our attic. It's a treasured memento. When we celebrate our golden wedding anniversary, I'm going to tell our kids how you tricked me into marrying you. You'll see," he teased, "they'll point a finger at you and say, 'Shame, shame!' " He whipped one of Lance Trainor's cowboy hats from behind his back and plunked it on her head. "There."

Holly doubled up, laughing. "You do and I'll tell them the only reason you married me was to prove you have androgens."

He stretched out on the bed, gathering her in his arms. "How many children shall we have?"

A flush of joy thrilled her. She thought of the beautiful babies they'd make together, and the wonderful father he'd be. "Three," she decided, sensuously rubbing his bare leg. "A boy, a girl, and one to grow on."

He shook his head. "Unfair. We'll compromise. Two boys and two girls. No wigs. Straight blonds. The girls will look like you, and the boys will look like me."

"Deal," she agreed, then thought about her career. "Suppose I want to work? I might miss researching."

Then you'll work. I'd never stand in your way."

"And you won't boss me?" She twirled a hair on his chest.

"Never," he dutifully promised.

"Or make me drink a guggle muggle."

"Don't press your luck," he warned.

Holly knew when to retreat. Steven would probably go on bossing her until the day she died. She'd go on resisting, when she wanted to, and giving in some of the time. It was called compromise. It was also called love.

"I won't," she promised.

He smiled, knowing they'd have a wonderful life. Holly would let him get away with just so much; then he'd retreat. It was called compromise. It was, he supposed, the secret of a happy marriage.

"Where's your juice?" she asked, thinking of all the breakfasts to come.

"Don't need it."

"Why not?"

Actually, he'd had his in the kitchen, but he wanted to tease her. "Androgens, remember?"

They'd made love all night, and each time was more wonderful, more exciting.

"Are you ever going to let me forget that?" She sat up, exposing a coral-tipped breast. Before she could pull up the sheet, his mouth covered the satiny flesh, suckling until she moaned.

"Never," he said, kissing her other breast. "I like this cruel and unusual form of punishment."

"Androgens, hmmmm? Care to prove it again?"

He was already reaching for her. "What'll you give me if I do?"

She loved his deep, rich voice. Especially when it became husky, as now.

"Me," she promised.

She watched him slowly remove the towel. She obligingly removed the ridiculous brown wig from his head.

"Now, where were we?" he asked, tossing his cowboy hat carelessly on a chair.

"I think this is the part where I show you a thing or two," she teased.

His eyes darkened to a smoldering blue. "Do your worst," he commanded. "I can resist anything."

"Like this?" she whispered, finding him with a kiss. She caught him off guard.

His voice roughened. "You're a fast learner."

She met the surprised look in his eyes with satisfaction. "I have a good teacher."

"Your lessons aren't over."

She shimmied slowly up the length of his body, kissing him. "What do you want to do today?"

He touched her, making her gasp. "A little of this," he murmured, keeping up the sweet torture, "and a little of that."

She moved her hand, hearing him moan. Her voice was husky. "Why don't we start with a little of this?"

They spent the morning in bed, making love. The phone rang four times; each time they pulled the blankets over their heads like two naughty children, giggling like mad till it stopped ringing.

Steven taught her that making love could be fun, it could be slow and sensual, or it could be fast and violent—each time different, each time sending her to the edge of madness.

When it was past noon, Steven bounced out of bed, dragging the sheet with him. "Rise and shine, princess. I'm famished. I hope you know how to cook?"

"I'm a fabulous cook, and you know it. Since you were so nice to me, I'll make you oatmeal," she teased, getting a predictable reaction.

"What! I take back my offer. I will not go through life without bacon and eggs. And hash browns . . . and sourdough biscuits . . . and—"

"Are you marrying me for my culinary arts?"

He rubbed the side of his jaw, thinking. "I don't know," he said, pretending to pout. "You've given me cause for alarm; I might take back my offer."

"In that case, you big baby, we'll both fix breakfast. I'll make the bacon and eggs, you set the table."

She eyed the mess in the room. It resembled a war zone, with Steven's clothes on the floor, Lance Trainor's hat on the edge of a chair, and her wig sticking out from beneath the bed. Steven saw the frown on her face.

"Don't worry about it," he said, characteristically nonchalant about the chaos. "Hortense will clean up. She's coming tomorrow."

"No, she's not," Holly answered, before she had a chance to think.

Steven popped his head back into the room. He had been on his way to the shower when he'd heard the low-spoken remark. An itch behind his neck made him double back into the room. "How do *you* know she's not coming?"

"I have it on good authority," Holly said airily,

"that Hortense will be quitting her job. You see, she's about to be married."

He swore softly. There was a menacing gleam in his eye. "Married, you say?"

Holly pointed to the third finger on her left hand, wiggling it for effect. With a half-laugh, in a voice fraught with meaning, she said, "I was just going to explain about Hortense."

Steven advanced toward the bed, suspicion written all over his features. "What does she plan to do with her grown children—take them with her on her honeymoon?"

Holly took one look at him and scrambled for the sheet; Steven's foot came down hard, preventing her from picking it up from the floor. She lay there, defenseless and shaking with mirth. This wasn't the way she had envisioned telling Steven he'd be losing a maid.

"Oh, dear," she cried helplessly. "Now I suppose you won't want to marry me. After all, good maids are harder to find than good wives, aren't they, darling?"

Steven let his gaze drop. The taste of passion began to ripple through him. "I suppose this is another one of Digger's inspirations?"

"Yes—one of his more rotten ones, I might add. Darling, you *really* leave a mess."

"Those notes!" Steven thundered. "*You* left me those notes. *You* even charged me double, you little minx. I expect a refund."

Holly bent over to try to cover herself with the sheet. It still didn't budge. "I should have charged you triple," she panted. "If it weren't for me, Digger would have planted a real spy in your home. Then where would you have been?"

Bending his knee, he leaned on the bed, pulling her back with him. "Probably at my lawyer's. There's a law against that sort of trespassing."

"That's what Mark said. He offered you free counsel."

"Very astute fellow, your brother." Steven captured Holly's arms and held them above her head. She was flat out on the bed, helpless. "We'll have to phone him later and invite him to go with us to Marte Cudworth's."

"You're still planning on going? Digger will be there."

"Of course we're going. It's the perfect place to announce our engagement. Louise and Larry are planning to go. Who knows? Maybe by then Louise and Larry will have a surprise of their own. Marte will be delighted. She loves a good romantic ending. Trish Cole will be there too. Mark ought to be happy about that."

Holly listened to the man who used to be the world's most confirmed bachelor. "You're a regular little matchmaker, aren't you?"

"Yup! Now," he asked with a gleam in his eye, "what should the little old matchmaker give you for your good deeds?"

"I don't know," she teased. "I'll think about it. Where's the merry-go-round? I liked it."

"I sent it to a children's hospital. If you like it so much, we'll buy another one. And don't change the subject. What do you want from me?"

"You," she said simply, showing him by the love in her eyes that she meant it.

"You know, Louise said I'd need three women to marry. I'll be damned—it's come true."

"Three women? What three women?" Holly didn't like the sound of Louise's advice. She planned on keeping Steven busy enough for ten women.

"You can ask her yourself at the party."

She would. Then she giggled. "Wait till Digger gets wind of this."

"I've got plans for Digger," Steven said. He lay half over her, nuzzling the sensitive spot behind her ear. "*Mmmm*. Delicious."

"What do you mean?" Holly asked nervously.

Amusement flared in Steven's eyes, and Holly breathed a sigh of relief.

"If it weren't for Digger, we wouldn't have met. You'd still be working behind the stacks in a library somewhere or other. The way I see it, I owe him an interview."

"You wouldn't!" Holly protested. She tried kicking her legs, only to have Steven throw his over them, locking them. "If that's the case, why don't I interview you?" She'd tear up the information before letting another woman near him!

There was a gleam of triumph in Steven's eyes. "Calm down, tiger, I haven't told you the rest. I'll answer every question—within reason, of course. Then I'll tell him he can't use the material. When he asks why, I'll simply tell him I'm off the market, because we're getting married. That oughta fix him."

Knowing Digger, Holly knew it was the perfect

revenge. He'd have to find another bachelor, and he'd be late for his deadline!

Holly slid her arms around Steven's neck. It was time to let her bones melt. "I love you, Steven William Chadwick."

In his eyes she saw the love, the strength, and the tender passion of the man she was about to marry.

"And I love you, Holly Elizabeth Anderson."

Then he proceeded to prove it.

THE EDITOR'S CORNER

What a wonderful summer of romance reading we have in store for you. Truly, you're going to be LOVESWEPT with some happy surprises through the long, hot, lazy days ahead.

First, you're going to get **POCKETS FULL OF JOY,** LOVESWEPT #270, by our new Canadian author, Judy Gill. Elaina McIvor wondered helplessly what she was going to do with an eleven-month-old baby to care for. Dr. "Brad" Bradshaw had been the stork and deposited the infant on her doorstep and raced away. But he was back soon enough to "play doctor" and "play house" in one of the most delightful and sensuous romances of the season.

Joan Elliott Pickart has created two of her most intriguing characters ever in **TATTERED WINGS,** LOVESWEPT #271. Devastatingly handsome Mark Hampton—an Air Force Colonel whose once exciting life now seems terribly lonely—and beautiful, enigmatic Eden Landry—a top fashion model who left her glamorous life for a secluded ranch—meet one snowy night. Desire flares immediately. But so do problems. Mark soon discovers that Eden is like a perfect butterfly encased in a cube of glass. You'll revel in the ways he finds to break down the walls without hurting the woman!

For all of you who've written to ask for Tara's and Jed's love story, here your fervent requests

(continued)

are answered with Barbara Boswell's terrific **AND TARA, TOO,** LOVESWEPT #272. As we know, Jed Ramsey is as darkly sleek and as seductive and as winning with women as a man can be. And Tara Brady wants no part of him. It would be just too convenient, she thinks, if all the Brady sisters married Ramsey men. But that's exactly what Jed's tyrannical father has in mind. You'll chuckle and gasp as Tara and Jed rattle the chains of fate in a breathlessly sensual and touching love story.

Margie McDonnell is an author who can transport you to another world. This time she takes you to **THE LAND OF ENCHANTMENT,** via LOVE-SWEPT #273, to meet a modern-day, ever so gallant knight, dashing Patrick Knight, and the sensitive and lovely Karen Harris. Karen is the single parent of an exceptional son and a quite sensible lady . . . until she falls for the handsome hunk who is as merry as he is creative. We think you'll delight in this very special, very thrilling love story.

It gives us enormous pleasure next month to celebrate the fifth anniversary of Iris Johansen's writing career. Her first ever published book was LOVESWEPT's **STORMY VOWS** in August 1983. With that and its companion romance **TEMPEST AT SEA,** published in September 1983, Iris launched the romance featuring spin-off and/or continuing characters. Now everyone's doing it! But, still,

(continued)

nobody does it quite like the woman who began it all, Iris Johansen. Here, next month, you'll meet old friends and new lovers in **BLUE SKIES AND SHINING PROMISES,** LOVESWEPT #274. (The following month she'll also have a LOVESWEPT, of course, and we wonder if you can guess who the featured characters will be.) Don't miss the thrilling love story of Cameron Bandor (yes, you know him) and Damita Shaughnessy, whose background will shock, surprise and move you, taking you right back to five years ago!

Welcome, back, Peggy Webb! In the utterly bewitching LOVESWEPT #275, **SLEEPLESS NIGHTS,** Peggy tells the story of Tanner Donovan of the quicksilver eyes and Amanda Lassiter of the tart tongue and tender heart. In this thrilling and sensuous story, you have a marvelous battle of wits between lovers parted in the past and determined to best each other in the present. A real delight!

As always, we hope that not one of our LOVE-SWEPTs will ever disappoint you. Enjoy!

Carolyn Nichols

Carolyn Nichols
    Editor
LOVESWEPT
Bantam Books
666 Fifth Avenue
New York, NY 10103

THE HOMETOWN HUNK CONTEST

FOR EVERY WOMAN WHO HAS EVER SAID—
"I know a man who looks
just like the hero of this book"
—HAVE WE GOT A CONTEST FOR YOU!

To help celebrate our fifth year of publishing LOVESWEPT we are having a fabulous, fun-filled event called THE HOMETOWN HUNK contest. We are going to reissue six classic early titles by six of your favorite authors.

> **DARLING OBSTACLES by Barbara Boswell**
> **IN A CLASS BY ITSELF by Sandra Brown**
> **C.J.'S FATE by Kay Hooper**
> **THE LADY AND THE UNICORN by Iris Johansen**
> **CHARADE by Joan Elliott Pickart**
> **FOR THE LOVE OF SAMI by Fayrene Preston**

Here, as in the backs of all July, August, and September 1988 LOVESWEPTS you will find "cover notes" just like the ones we prepare at Bantam as the background for our art director to create our covers. These notes will describe the hero and heroine, give a teaser on the plot, and suggest a scene for the cover. Your part in the contest will be to see if a great looking local man—or men, if your hometown is so blessed—fits our description of one of the heroes of the six books we will reissue.

THE HOMETOWN HUNK who is selected (one for each of the six titles) will be flown to New York via United Airlines and will stay at the Loews Summit Hotel—the ideal hotel for business or pleasure in midtown Manhattan—for two nights. All travel arrangements made by Reliable Travel International, Incorporated. He will be the model for the new cover of the book which will be released in mid-1989. The six people who send in the winning photos of their HOMETOWN HUNK will receive a pre-selected assortment of LOVESWEPT books free for one year. Please see the Official Rules above the Official Entry Form for full details and restrictions.

We can't wait to start judging those pictures! Oh, and you must let the man you've chosen know that you're entering him in the contest. After all, if he wins he'll have to come to New York.

Have fun. Here's your chance to get the cover-lover of your dreams!

Carolyn Nichols

Carolyn Nichols
Editor
LOVESWEPT
Bantam Books
666 Fifth Avenue
New York, NY 10102—0023

THE HOMETOWN HUNK CONTEST

DARLING OBSTACLES
(Originally Published as LOVESWEPT #95)
By Barbara Boswell

COVER NOTES

The Characters:

Hero:
GREG WILDER's gorgeous body and "to-die-for" good looks haven't hurt him in the dating department, but when most women discover he's a widower with four kids, they head for the hills! Greg has the hard, muscular build of an athlete, and his light brown hair, which he wears neatly parted on the side, is streaked blond by the sun. Add to that his aquamarine blue eyes that sparkle when he laughs, and his sensual mouth and generous lower lip, and you're probably wondering what woman in her right mind wouldn't want Greg's strong, capable surgeon's hands working their magic on her—kids or no kids!

Personality Traits:
An acclaimed neurosurgeon, Greg Wilder is a celebrity of sorts in the planned community of Woodland, Maryland. Authoritative, debonair, self-confident, his reputation for engaging in one casual relationship after another almost overshadows his prowess as a doctor. In reality, Greg dates more out of necessity than anything else, since he has to attend one social function after another. He considers most of the events boring and wishes he could spend more time with his children. But his profession is a difficult and demanding one—and being both father and mother to four kids isn't any less so. A thoughtful, generous, sometimes befuddled father, Greg tries to do it all. Cerebral, he uses his intellect and skill rather than physical strength to win his victories. However, he never expected to come up against one Mary Magdalene May!

Heroine:
MARY MAGDALENE MAY, called Maggie by her friends, is the thirty-two-year-old mother of three children. She has shoulder-length auburn hair, and green eyes that shout her Irish heritage. With high cheekbones and an upturned nose covered with a smattering of freckles, Maggie thinks of herself more as the girl-next-door type. Certainly, she believes, she could never be one of Greg Wilder's beautiful escorts.

Setting: The small town of Woodland, Maryland

The Story:
Surgeon Greg Wilder wanted to court the feisty and beautiful widow who'd been caring for his four kids, but she just wouldn't let him past her doorstep! Sure that his interest was only casual, and that he preferred more sophisticated women, Maggie May vowed to keep Greg at arm's length. But he wouldn't take no for an answer. And once he'd crashed through her defenses and pulled her into his arms, he was tireless—and reckless—in his campaign to win her over. Maggie had found it tough enough to resist one determined doctor; now he threatened to call in his kids and hers as reinforcements—seven rowdy snags to romance!

Cover scene:
As if romancing Maggie weren't hard enough, Greg can't seem to find time to spend with her without their children around. Stealing a private moment on the stairs in Maggie's house, Greg and Maggie embrace. She is standing one step above him, but she still has to look up at him to see into his eyes. Greg's hands are on her hips, and her hands are resting on his shoulders. Maggie is wearing a very sheer, short pink nightgown, and Greg has on wheat-colored jeans and a navy and yellow striped rugby shirt. Do they have time to kiss?

THE HOMETOWN HUNK CONTEST

IN A CLASS BY ITSELF
(Originally Published as LOVESWEPT #66)
By Sandra Brown

COVER NOTES

The Characters:

Hero:
LOGAN WEBSTER would have no trouble posing for a Scandinavian travel poster. His wheat-colored hair always seems to be tousled, defying attempts to control it, and falls across his wide forehead. Thick eyebrows one shade darker than his hair accentuate his crystal blue eyes. He has a slender nose that flairs slightly over a mouth that testifies to both sensitivity and strength. The faint lines around his eyes and alongside his mouth give the impression that reaching the ripe age of 30 wasn't all fun and games for him. Logan's square, determined jaw is punctuated by a vertical cleft. His broad shoulders and narrow waist add to his tall, lean appearance.

Personality traits:
Logan Webster has had to scrape and save and fight for everything he's gotten. Born into a poor farm family, he was driven to succeed and overcome his "wrong side of the tracks" image. His businesses include cattle, real estate, and natural gas. Now a pillar of the community, Logan's life has been a true rags-to-riches story. Only Sandra Brown's own words can describe why he is masculinity epitomized: "Logan had 'the walk,' that saddle-tramp saunter that was inherent to native Texan men, passed down through generations of cowboys. It was, without even trying to be, sexy. The unconscious roll of the hips, the slow strut, the flexed knees, the slouching stance, the deceptive laziness that hid a latent aggressiveness." Wow! And not only does he have "the walk," but he's fun

and generous and kind. Even with his wealth, he feels at home living in his small hometown with simple, hard-working, middle-class, backbone-of-America folks. A born leader, people automatically gravitate toward him.

Heroine:
DANI QUINN is a sophisticated twenty-eight-year-old woman. Dainty, her body compact, she is utterly feminine. Dani's pale, lustrous hair is moonlight and honey spun together, and because it is very straight, she usually wears it in a chignon. With golden eyes to match her golden hair, Dani is the one woman Logan hasn't been able to get off his mind for the ten years they've been apart.

Setting: Primarily on Logan's ranch in East Texas.

The Story:
Ten years had passed since Dani Quinn had graduated from high school in the small Texas town, ten years since the night her elopement with Logan Webster had ended in disaster. Now Dani approached her tenth reunion with uncertainty. Logan would be there . . . Logan, the only man who'd ever made her shiver with desire and need, but would she have the courage to face the fury in his eyes? She couldn't defend herself against his anger and hurt—to do so would demand she reveal the secret sorrow she shared with no one. Logan's touch had made her his so long ago. Could he reach past the pain to make her his for all time?

Cover Scene:
It's sunset, and Logan and Dani are standing beside the swimming pool on his ranch, embracing. The pool is surrounded by semitropical plants and lush flower beds. In the distance, acres of rolling pasture land resembling a green lake undulate into dense, piney woods. Dani is wearing a strapless, peacock blue bikini and sandals with leather ties that wrap around her ankles. Her hair is straight and loose, falling to the middle of her back. Logan has on a light-colored pair of corduroy shorts and a short-sleeved designer knit shirt in a pale shade of yellow.

THE HOMETOWN HUNK CONTEST

C.J.'S FATE
(Originally Published as LOVESWEPT #32)
By Kay Hooper

COVER NOTES

The Characters:

Hero:

FATE WESTON easily could have walked straight off an Indian reservation. His raven black hair and strong, well-molded features testify to his heritage. But somewhere along the line genetics threw Fate a curve—his eyes are the deepest, darkest blue imaginable! Above those blue eyes are dark slanted eyebrows, and fanning out from those eyes are faint laugh lines—the only sign of the fact that he's thirty-four years old. Tall, Fate moves with easy, loose-limbed grace. Although he isn't an athlete, Fate takes very good care of himself, and it shows in his strong physique. Striking at first glance and fascinating with each succeeding glance, the serious expressions on his face make him look older than his years, but with one smile he looks boyish again.

Personality traits:

Fate possesses a keen sense of humor. His heavy-lidded, intelligent eyes are capable of concealment, but there is a shrewdness in them that reveals the man hadn't needed college or a law degree to be considered intelligent. The set of his head tells you that he is proud—perhaps even a bit arrogant. He is attractive and perfectly well aware of that fact. Unconventional, paradoxical, tender, silly, lusty, gentle, comical, serious, absurd, and endearing are all words that come to mind when you think of Fate. He is not ashamed to be everything a man can be. A defense attorney by profession, one can detect a bit of frustrated actor in his character. More than anything else, though, it's the impression of humor about him—reinforced by the elusive dimple in his cheek—that makes Fate Weston a scrumptious hero!

Heroine:
C.J. ADAMS is a twenty-six-year-old research librarian. Unaware of her own attractiveness, C.J. tends to play down her pixylike figure and tawny gold eyes. But once she meets Fate, she no longer feels that her short, burnished copper curls and the sprinkling of freckles on her nose make her unappealing. He brings out the vixen in her, and changes the smart, bookish woman who professed to have no interest in men into the beautiful, sexy woman she really was all along. Now, if only he could get her to tell him what C.J. stands for!

Setting: Ski lodge in Aspen, Colorado

The Story:
C.J. Adams had been teased enough about her seeming lack of interest in the opposite sex. On a ski trip with her five best friends, she impulsively embraced a handsome stranger, pretending they were secret lovers—and the delighted lawyer who joined in her impetuous charade seized the moment to deepen the kiss. Astonished at his reaction, C.J. tried to nip their romance in the bud—but found herself nipping at his neck instead! She had met her match in a man who could answer her witty remarks with clever ripostes of his own, and a lover whose caresses aroused in her a passionate need she'd never suspected that she could feel. Had destiny somehow tossed them together?

Cover Scene:
C.J. and Fate virtually have the ski slopes to themselves early one morning, and they take advantage of it! Frolicking in a snow drift, Fate is covering C.J. with snow—and kisses! They are flushed from the cold weather and from the excitement of being in love. C.J. is wearing a sky-blue, one-piece, tight-fitting ski outfit that zips down the front. Fate is wearing a navy blue parka and matching ski pants.

THE HOMETOWN HUNK CONTEST

THE LADY AND THE UNICORN
(Originally Published as LOVESWEPT #29)
By Iris Johansen

COVER NOTES

The Characters:

Hero:
Not classically handsome, RAFE SANTINE's blunt, craggy features reinforce the quality of overpowering virility about him. He has wide, Slavic cheekbones and a bold, thrusting chin, which give the impression of strength and authority. Thick black eyebrows are set over piercing dark eyes. He wears his heavy, dark hair long. His large frame measures in at almost six feet four inches, and it's hard to believe that a man with such brawny shoulders and strong thighs could exhibit the pantherlike grace which characterizes Rafe's movements. Rafe Santine is definitely a man to be reckoned with, and heroine Janna Cannon does just that!

Personality traits:
Our hero is a man who radiates an aura of power and danger, and women find him intriguing and irresistible. Rafe Santine is a self-made billionaire at the age of thirty-eight. Almost entirely self-educated, he left school at sixteen to work on his first construction job, and by the time he was twenty-three, he owned the company. From there he branched out into real estate, computers, and oil. Rafe reportedly changes mistresses as often as he changes shirts. His reputation for ruthless brilliance has been earned over years of fighting to the top of the economic ladder from the slums of New York. His gruff manner and hard personality hide the tender, vulnerable side of him. Rafe also possesses an insatiable thirst for knowledge that is a passion with him. Oddly enough, he has a wry sense of

humor that surfaces unexpectedly from time to time. And, though cynical to the extreme, he never lets his natural skepticism interfere with his innate sense of justice.

Heroine:
JANNA CANNON, a game warden for a small wildlife preserve, is a very dedicated lady. She is tall at five feet nine inches and carries herself in a stately way. Her long hair is dark brown and is usually twisted into a single thick braid in back. Of course, Rafe never lets her keep her hair braided when they make love! Janna is one quarter Cherokee Indian by heritage, and she possesses the dark eyes and skin of her ancestors.

Setting: Rafe's estate in Carmel, California

The Story:
Janna Cannon scaled the high walls of Rafe Santine's private estate, afraid of nothing and determined to appeal to the powerful man who could save her beloved animal preserve. She bewitched his guard dogs, then cast a spell of enchantment over him as well. Janna's profound grace, her caring nature, made the tough and proud Rafe grow mercurial in her presence. She offered him a gift he'd never risked reaching out for before—but could he trust his own emotions enough to open himself to her love?

Cover Scene:
In the gazebo overlooking the rugged cliffs at the edge of the Pacific Ocean, Rafe and Janna share a passionate moment together. The gazebo is made of redwood and the interior is small and cozy. Scarlet cushions cover the benches, and matching scarlet curtains hang from the eaves, caught back by tasseled sashes to permit the sea breeze to whip through the enclosure. Rafe is wearing black suede pants and a charcoal gray crew-neck sweater. Janna is wearing a safari-style khaki shirt-and-slacks outfit and suede desert boots. They embrace against the breathtaking backdrop of wild, crashing, white-crested waves pounding the rocks and cliffs below.

THE HOMETOWN HUNK CONTEST

CHARADE
(Originally Published as LOVESWEPT #74)
By Joan Elliott Pickart

COVER NOTES

The Characters:

Hero:
The phrase tall, dark, and handsome was coined to describe TENNES WHITNEY. His coal black hair reaches past his collar in back, and his fathomless steel gray eyes are framed by the kind of thick, dark lashes that a woman would kill to have. Darkly tanned, Tennes has a straight nose and a square chin, with—you guessed it!—a Kirk Douglas cleft. Tennes oozes masculinity and virility. He's a handsome son-of-a-gun!

Personality traits:
A shrewd, ruthless business tycoon, Tennes is a man of strength and principle. He's perfected the art of buying floundering companies and turning them around financially, then selling them at a profit. He possesses a sixth sense about business—in short, he's a winner! But there are two sides to his personality. Always in cool command, Tennes, who fears no man or challenge, is rendered emotionally vulnerable when faced with his elderly aunt's illness. His deep devotion to the woman who raised him clearly casts him as a warm, compassionate guy—not at all like the tough-as-nails executive image he presents. Leave it to heroine Whitney Jordan to discover the real man behind the complicated enigma.

Heroine:
WHITNEY JORDAN's russet-colored hair floats past her shoulders in glorious waves. Her emerald green eyes, full breasts, and long, slender legs—not to mention her peaches-

and-cream complexion—make her eye-poppingly attractive. How can Tennes resist the twenty-six-year-old beauty? And how can Whitney consider becoming serious with him? If their romance flourishes, she may end up being Whitney Whitney!

Setting: Los Angeles, California

The Story:
One moment writer Whitney Jordan was strolling the aisles of McNeil's Department Store, plotting the untimely demise of a soap opera heartthrob; the next, she was nearly knocked over by a real-life stunner who implored her to be his fiancée! The ailing little gray-haired aunt who'd raised him had one final wish, he said—to see her dear nephew Tennes married to the wonderful girl he'd described in his letters . . . only that girl hadn't existed—until now! Tennes promised the masquerade would last only through lunch, but Whitney gave such an inspired performance that Aunt Olive refused to let her go. And what began as a playful romantic deception grew more breathlessly real by the minute. . . .

Cover Scene:
Whitney's living room is bright and cheerful. The gray carpeting and blue sofa with green and blue throw pillows gives the apartment a cool but welcoming appearance. Sitting on the sofa next to Tennes, Whitney is wearing a black crepe dress that is simply cut but stunning. It is cut low over her breasts and held at the shoulders by thin straps. The skirt falls to her knees in soft folds and the bodice is nipped in at the waist with a matching belt. She has on black high heels, but prefers not to wear any jewelry to spoil the simplicity of the dress. Tennes is dressed in a black suit with a white silk shirt and a deep red tie.

THE HOMETOWN HUNK CONTEST

FOR THE LOVE OF SAMI
(Originally Published as LOVESWEPT #34)
By Fayrene Preston

COVER NOTES

Hero:
DANIEL PARKER-ST. JAMES is every woman's dream come true. With glossy black hair and warm, reassuring blue eyes, he makes our heroine melt with just a glance. Daniel's lean face is chiseled into assertive planes. His lips are full and firmly sculptured, and his chin has the determined and arrogant thrust to it only a man who's sure of himself can carry off. Daniel has a lot in common with Clark Kent. Both wear glasses, and when Daniel removes them to make love to Sami, she thinks he really is Superman!

Personality traits:
Daniel Parker-St. James is one of the Twin Cities' most respected attorneys. He's always in the news, either in the society columns with his latest society lady, or on the front page with his headline cases. He's brilliant and takes on only the toughest cases—usually those that involve millions of dollars. Daniel has a reputation for being a deadly opponent in the courtroom. Because he's from a socially prominent family and is a Harvard graduate, it's expected that he'll run for the Senate one day. Distinguished-looking and always distinctively dressed—he's fastidious about his appearance—Daniel gives off an unassailable air of authority and absolute control.

Heroine:
SAMUELINA (SAMI) ADKINSON is secretly a wealthy heiress. No one would guess. She lives in a converted warehouse loft, dresses to suit no one but herself, and dabbles in the creative arts. Sami is twenty-six years old, with

long, honey-colored hair. She wears soft, wispy bangs and has very thick brown lashes framing her golden eyes. Of medium height, Sami has to look up to gaze into Daniel's deep blue eyes.

Setting: St. Paul, Minnesota

The Story:
Unpredictable heiress Sami Adkinson had endeared herself to the most surprising people—from the bag ladies in the park she protected . . . to the mobster who appointed himself her guardian . . . to her exasperated but loving friends. Then Sami was arrested while demonstrating to save baby seals, and it took powerful attorney Daniel Parker-St. James to bail her out. Daniel was smitten, soon cherishing Sami and protecting her from her night fears. Sami reveled in his love—and resisted it too. And holding on to Sami, Daniel discovered, was like trying to hug quicksilver. . . .

Cover Scene:
The interior of Daniel's house is very grand and supremely formal, the decor sophisticated, refined, and quietly tasteful, just like Daniel himself. Rich traditional fabrics cover plush oversized custom sofas and Regency wing chairs. Queen Anne furniture is mixed with Chippendale and is subtly complemented with Oriental accent pieces. In the library, floor-to-ceiling bookcases filled with rare books provide the backdrop for Sami and Daniel's embrace. Sami is wearing a gold satin sheath gown. The dress has a high neckline, but in back is cut provocatively to the waist. Her jewels are exquisite. The necklace is made up of clusters of flowers created by large, flawless diamonds. From every cluster a huge, perfectly matched teardrop emerald hangs. The earrings are composed of an even larger flower cluster, and an equally huge teardrop-shaped emerald hangs from each one. Daniel is wearing a classic, elegant tuxedo.

LOVESWEPT® HOMETOWN HUNK CONTEST

OFFICIAL RULES

> IN A CLASS BY ITSELF by Sandra Brown
> FOR THE LOVE OF SAMI by Fayrene Preston
> C.J.'S FATE by Kay Hooper
> THE LADY AND THE UNICORN by Iris Johansen
> CHARADE by Joan Elliott Pickart
> DARLING OBSTACLES by Barbara Boswell

1. NO PURCHASE NECESSARY. Enter the HOMETOWN HUNK contest by completing the Official Entry Form below and enclosing a sharp color full-length photograph (easy to see details, with the photo being no smaller than 2½″ × 3½″) of the man you think perfectly represents one of the heroes from the above-listed books which are described in the accompanying Loveswept cover notes. Please be sure to fill out the Official Entry Form completely, and also be sure to clearly print on the back of the man's photograph the man's name, address, city, state, zip code, telephone number, date of birth, your name, address, city, state, zip code, telephone number, your relationship, if any, to the man (e.g. wife, girlfriend) as well as the title of the Loveswept book for which you are entering the man. If you do not have an Official Entry Form, you can print all of the required information on a 3″ × 5″ card and attach it to the photograph with all the necessary information printed on the back of the photograph as well. YOUR HERO MUST SIGN BOTH THE BACK OF THE OFFICIAL ENTRY FORM (OR 3″ × 5″ CARD) AND THE PHOTOGRAPH TO SIGNIFY HIS CONSENT TO BEING ENTERED IN THE CONTEST. Completed entries should be sent to:

> BANTAM BOOKS
> HOMETOWN HUNK CONTEST
> Department CN
> 666 Fifth Avenue
> New York, New York 10102–0023

All photographs and entries become the property of Bantam Books and will not be returned under any circumstances.

2. Six men will be chosen by the Loveswept authors as a HOMETOWN HUNK (one HUNK per Loveswept title). By entering the contest, each winner and each person who enters a winner agrees to abide by Bantam Books' rules and to be subject to Bantam Books' eligibility requirements. Each winning HUNK and each person who enters a winner will be required to sign all papers deemed necessary by Bantam Books before receiving any prize. Each winning HUNK will be flown via **United Airlines** from his closest United Airlines-serviced city to New York City and will stay at the ▂▎**S**t**NN**rr Hotel—the ideal hotel for business or pleasure in midtown Manhattan—for two nights. Winning HUNKS' meals and hotel transfers will be provided by Bantam Books. Travel and hotel arrangements are made by *RELIABLE TRAVEL* ▪▪▪▪▪ and are subject to availability and to Bantam Books' date requirements. Each winning HUNK will pose with a female model at a photographer's studio for a photograph that will serve as the basis of a Loveswept front cover. Each winning HUNK will receive a $150.00 modeling fee. Each winning HUNK will be required to sign an Affidavit of Eligibility and Model's Release supplied by Bantam Books. (Approximate retail value of HOMETOWN HUNK'S PRIZE: $900.00). The six people who send in a winning HOMETOWN HUNK photograph that is used by Bantam will receive free for one year each, LOVESWEPT romance paperback books published by Bantam during that year. (Approximate retail value: $180.00.) Each person who submits a winning photograph

will also be required to sign an Affidavit of Eligibility and Promotional Release supplied by Bantam Books. All winning HUNKS' (as well as the people who submit the winning photographs) names, addresses, biographical data and likenesses may be used by Bantam Books for publicity and promotional purposes without any additional compensation. There will be no prize substitutions or cash equivalents made.

3. All completed entries must be received by Bantam Books no later than September 15, 1988. Bantam Books is not responsible for lost or misdirected entries. The finalists will be selected by Loveswept editors and the six winning HOMETOWN HUNKS will be selected by the six authors of the participating Loveswept books. Winners will be selected on the basis of how closely the judges believe they reflect the descriptions of the books' heroes. Winners will be notified on or about October 31, 1988. If there are insufficient entries or if in the judges' opinions, no entry is suitable or adequately reflects the descriptions of the hero(s) in the book(s), Bantam may decide not to award a prize for the applicable book(s) and may reissue the book(s) at its discretion.

4. The contest is open to residents of the U.S. and Canada, except the Province of Quebec, and is void where prohibited by law. All federal and local regulations apply. Employees of Reliable Travel International, Inc., United Airlines, the Summit Hotel, and the Bantam Doubleday Dell Publishing Group, Inc., their subsidiaries and affiliates, and their immediate families are ineligible to enter.

5. For an extra copy of the Official Rules, the Official Entry Form, and the accompanying Loveswept cover notes, send your request and a self-addressed stamped envelope (Vermont and Washington State residents need not affix postage) before August 20, 1988 to the address listed in Paragraph 1 above.

LOVESWEPT ® HOMETOWN HUNK OFFICIAL ENTRY FORM

BANTAM BOOKS
HOMETOWN HUNK CONTEST
Dept. CN
666 Fifth Avenue
New York, New York 10102-0023

HOMETOWN HUNK CONTEST

YOUR NAME_____

YOUR ADDRESS_____

CITY_____ STATE_____ ZIP_____

THE NAME OF THE LOVESWEPT BOOK FOR WHICH YOU ARE ENTERING THIS PHOTO

_____by_____

YOUR RELATIONSHIP TO YOUR HERO_____

YOUR HERO'S NAME_____

YOUR HERO'S ADDRESS_____

CITY_____ STATE_____ ZIP_____

YOUR HERO'S TELEPHONE #_____

YOUR HERO'S DATE OF BIRTH_____

YOUR HERO'S SIGNATURE CONSENTING TO HIS PHOTOGRAPH ENTRY

_____

THE DELANEY DYNASTY

Men and women whose loves and passions are so glorious it takes many great romance novels by three bestselling authors to tell their tempestuous stories.

THE SHAMROCK TRINITY

THE DELANEYS OF KILLAROO

Now Available!
THE DELANEYS: *The Untamed Years*

Buy these books at your local bookstore or use the handy coupon below.

Prices and availability subject to change without notice.

- -

Special Offer
Buy a Bantam Book
for only 50¢.

Now you can have Bantam's catalog filled with hundreds of titles plus take advantage of our unique and exciting bonus book offer. A special offer which gives you the opportunity to purchase a Bantam book for only 50¢. Here's how!

By ordering any five books at the regular price per order, you can also choose any other single book listed (up to a $5.95 value) for just 50¢. Some restrictions do apply, but for further details why not send for Bantam's catalog of titles today!

Just send us your name and address and we will send you a catalog!